BY IMPERIAL DECREE

ESTO Universe

ANGEL MARTINEZ

Edited by
JUDE DUNN
Cover by
FREDDY MACKAY

COPYRIGHT

About the Book You Have Purchased:

This copy is intended for the original purchaser of this book ONLY. No part of this book may be reproduced, scanned, or distributed in any printed or electronic form without prior written permission from the authors. Please do not participate in or encourage piracy of copyrighted materials in violation of the author's rights. Purchase only authorized editions.

Cover Artist: Freddy MacKay
Editor: Jude Dunn

First Edition
BY IMPERIAL DECREE: ESTO UNIVERSE © 2020 Angel Martinez
All Rights Reserved.
Published in the United States of America.

ALL RIGHTS RESERVED: *By Imperial Decree* is a work of fiction. Names, places, characters, and incidents are either the product of the author's imagination or are fictionalized. Any resemblance to any actual persons, living or dead, is entirely coincidental. The story contains explicit sexual content and is intended for adult readers.

Any person depicted in the Licensed Art Material is a model and is being used solely for illustrative purposes.

PUBLISHER
Mischief Corner Books, LLC

An Imperial prince can only hide for so long— but his solution of a hastily invented engagement could backfire spectacularly.

Marsh Kensinger's work as the utility mechanic for Bremen Station keeps his life interesting - but never quite as interesting as finding a pilot still hidden inside a hibernation drawer in what should have been a salvage craft. He knows he shouldn't get involved, but the Altairian Imperial crest on the private craft and the semi-conscious pilot's odd questions pique his always-whirling curiosity.

Still unattached at a concerning age for an imperial son, Prince Shiro Shinohara hadn't been running from the endless, mind-numbing rounds of *omiai* his mother, the Empress, had mandated. Not exactly. He'd just wanted a break from persistent suitors at the family retreat on Ceti Tau. The short respite becomes a panicked flight for his life when one of the suitors stalking him attacks the family compound.

Worried for the soldiers he was forced to leave behind, afraid there's a conspiracy to kidnap him, Shiro confides in the handsome mechanic who found him and in a moment of panic, concocts the fiction of a serious relationship with Marsh. It's only until Shiro's people can reach him and he can press charges back home. Marsh is willing to play along and Shiro's just going to have to keep himself together and not, under any circumstances, fall for the wonderful, generous man who refuses to stop helping him.

TABLE OF CONTENTS

DEDICATION

For my patient readers—the ones who always ask for more.

CHAPTER ONE

Dried cranberries came tucked beside the rice porridge that morning. Marsh checked the dispenser history in his quarters. No, he hadn't requested anything beyond his normal meal items. He didn't have a note in there from Medical for supplemental dietary requirements. Weird. Maybe someone in Culinary had found a forgotten stockpile from a holiday shipment.

Marsh shrugged, dumped the cranberries in the porridge, and ate in civilized bites instead of shoveling his breakfast in. *No rush. Take your time.*

The reminder had become a mantra, one he had been repeating every day for the last year. He no longer lived in the Journey Mechanics' quarters, four to a room. He no longer had to stagger out of bed early in the morning after shifts that ran over, no longer had to hurry, hurry, hurry, since there were four people using one dispenser and one hygiene facility, and no longer had to rush to make it to shift changes in Maintenance Control.

His schedule for the day popped up just as he'd settled in to read the station bulletins.

1. Salvage Bay 12, see Supervisor Kaneer

Marsh blinked at the single line—his entire schedule for the day. *Huh.* That could mean something complicated, or it could mean he just wasn't needed anywhere else that day. It happened, but only twice since he'd accepted the new position. He shrugged and dismissed his schedule. Most likely other things would come up.

"Gally, check the hydrometers on the plants before we leave today." When his AI ferret scampered over, he bent and booped their nose. "And run the minisweep, please."

As a child, he'd always had a mouse AI companion, but a ferret made more practical sense living on his own. He'd needed an AI who could reach sensors and press them for household tasks. Also, ferrets were adorable, galumphing and scurrying around. Gally investigated corners and scrabbled under counters, always searching for anything out of place, while Marsh pulled a blue coverall from the clean bin.

The apartment node chimed, the five climbing notes of his mothers' arpeggio, and a message popped into the air above the bed.

Did you fill out your needs assessment this month?

He tapped out a quick *Yes, Moms* with an exasperated snort, which made Gally stop exploring to *meep* at him. "Nothing. Sorry."

They would probably always worry. Maybe he should've taken the job on the *Shetland* instead of staying onstation. A mega barge wasn't the most exciting ship assignment, but at least his mothers would have been worrying a little farther away most of the time.

No, it's fine. I like having them close. Maybe if I did some crafting or joined a social group, they wouldn't worry as much. Which always sounds good in my head... I'd rather stay here and read. Speaking of...

Plenty of time still to check messages on the Pangalactic Book Club. They tended to have several reads going at once, and since the last time Marsh had checked a few days ago, it looked like an active argument had stirred up over the one he hadn't read yet, *Newt's Garden.*

Terpsichore: Too much dissonance between the fantasy elements and the apocalyptic setting

Redmaus: In what respect?

Terpsichore: The anthropomorphic characters belong in a children's picture book, not in a story about rebuilding a social structure after disaster. I found the simple language off-putting too.

Redmaus: It's reminiscent of old Earth fables in that respect and allows the story to be told as a fable, as a metaphor, with that one remove of fantasy characters.

TeaHerbert: I hated the cover.

The discussion went on without TeaHerbert, which it often did. Marsh wondered, as he had many times, who these people were, what their lives were like. Everyone in book club discussed under pseudonyms for privacy, but he couldn't help making up stories about the members sometimes. Redmaus was his favorite—always patient and polite, though with definite opinions that Marsh agreed with most of the time.

A chime brought him back to himself, letting him know it was time to get moving. He'd have to dig into what else Redmaus had been discussing later. *One quick response, just so they know I'm still out here.*

Stationbookworm: Sounds like something I'd enjoy. Have to start on it after work.

Redmaus didn't answer right away. Disappointing, but Marsh couldn't expect to be the center of the universe for a person he'd never met. If he thought about it too hard—the fact that he looked forward to talking to someone he only knew through text conversations more than the people he saw in real life —he'd just get depressed.

He pressed the spot beside his right knee, his limbnet humming through its ponderous start-up sequence. Central Supply had his application for a new rig, but they had to prioritize immediate needs. His still worked fine once it got going, nothing urgent. Little prickles ran up both legs as the net came online, and Marsh stood slowly to be sure of his balance and joints.

Still good.

Dressed, breakfast cleaned up, he stomped into his work boots and grabbed his tool pack. "I shouldn't need you this morning, Gally, but I'll come back for you if I do. Be good today."

Silly thing to say. Gally's programming ensured their best behavior when he was at work or asleep, with only little bouts of ferret behavior otherwise. Marsh shook his head at himself as he secured his quarters, then he powered up the mag-lev on his boots and skated off to work. The transport tubes were great for getting somewhere onstation fast, but most days he took the corridors, now that he could take his time.

Though he did have to get all the way to Ring Five, so he couldn't delay too much.

He glided silently through the E-4 habitat hallways, past his neighbors' doors, past the mini-gardens at each cross corridor and up the ramp to the E-5 level. From there, he only had a short skate to the concourse leading to Ring Four, and there he did stop for a few precious minutes. The concourse offered a 270-degree view of outside. It made a lot of stationers dizzy, which was why they took the tubes. Marsh tipped his head back and drank it in.

All those stars. All the ships coming and going. Bremen Station was the only home he'd ever known, the only place he'd ever been, and he didn't have any illusions about how dependent he was on its rhythms and its environment. His daydreams still flung him out into the stars, though. To go out with the ships and breathe a different air, to experience a different way of living he only glimpsed in vids—it was strange. Aching for things he'd never known.

An imperious beep startled him out of his thoughts of ships and far-flung planets. Marsh twisted around to find a yellow sweeper bot behind him. "Sorry, sorry. Didn't mean to block your route."

He stepped to the side and the bot tweeted a two-note *thank-you*, but the daydream spell had shattered. Marsh resettled his pack and skated off again.

After one more brief stop to admire his mothers' orange tree in the Ring Five apex courtyard, he made it to the salvage bay arm several minutes ahead of time. Supervisor Kaneer already stood beside a docked ship, probably the one in question, but he was almost certain she lived in the salvage bays.

She broke off scowling at the ship to offer him a smile. "Morning, Marsh."

"Morning, Mx. Kaneer. How can I help today?"

"Well. Not sure if you can." She waved a broad, scarred hand at the ship, a sleek twenty-five meter runabout of an unfamiliar design. "Hoping your love of unusual tech might help us. We think it's Altairian."

She thinks *it is?* "Um… where's the pilot?" He was afraid he knew the answer and wished he didn't have to hear it.

Instead, the answer shocked him. "We don't know."

Marsh blinked at her. "Oh?"

"The *Schipperke* found the ship adrift. Bio scans say it's empty, but it could be shielded." Supervisor Kaneer scratched at her bristle-short hair. "Problem is we can't get inside to check. We'll have to cut through the hull if we can't get it open."

Ah. Now the single item on his schedule made sense. Impossible to know how long this would take. "All right. Give me a few minutes and I should have a better idea."

She gave him a terse nod and strode off to the next ship along the bay, barking instructions to her mechanics as she went.

Scanner in hand, Marsh set his pack on the workbench and began a slow circuit of the hull. It certainly followed the basics of other Altairian designs —beautiful, fluid lines giving the appearance of seamless construction. There were echoes of Novasym fighters, those strange biotech creations that bonded symbiotically with their pilots, but this couldn't be one of those. At least, Marsh didn't think so. While sleek, it was too big for a two-man fighter.

He circled again, this time checking under the fins and stabilizers. *There.* Under the port fin lay a symbol etched in red—a stylized chrysanthemum. Part of the puzzle, anyway.

"Supervisor Kaneer?" Marsh straightened as she hurried over to crouch down and see where he pointed. "We've got an imperial noble's ship here."

Inventive cussing erupted from under the fin as she spotted the Altairian imperial crest. She straightened with a huff. "Fuck. Now we *can't* cut into it, and we'll have to wait for some hotshot flyboy from the empress's court to open it. I can't have this thing taking up a berth for weeks."

Marsh nodded absently. "Though maybe…"

Supervisor Kaneer raised an eyebrow at him and spun her hand in a *go-on* motion.

"The shape… it looks like a symbiont ship. It might have something like intelligence?"

"What're you planning on doing? Talking to it?"

"Um." Marsh cleared his throat, concentrating on the ship rather than her glower. "Yes, actually."

"You're serious." Her eyes narrowed, but she wasn't scoffing.

"I am. The ship probably responds to one specific pilot, but there has to be a way to open it in an emergency. I've read that some react to a set of keywords."

For a few heartbeats, Supervisor Kaneer still glowered. Then she gave him a sharp nod. "Fine.

Talk to the fancy, picky ship. I'll give you three hours."

Marsh pulled a crate over and put a hand on the ship's nose as he took a seat. "Hello, pretty ship. I hope you're listening, since we're just trying to get inside to see if we can find out what happened to you."

He pulled up the imperial family on his personal node and started reading off names. When he ran out of family members, he started listing imperial residences, then Altairian cities. He thought the ship quivered at Shikimi, but no door opened. Military ranks, victorious battles, and names of famous fleet admirals also resulted in no response.

But it's probably not a military ship. Maybe something more civilian oriented. He tried Altairian foods, then musical instruments. Nothing. Musicians. *Oh, crud, what if it's a song lyric? It could be anything.*

With half his allotted time remaining, though, giving up made no sense. Authors, poets, the first lines of some of the most revered Altairian poems— nothing. Since keywords could be something as simple as the owner's favorite color and names of pets, this didn't surprise Marsh. Still…

Artists. He started with painters just to start somewhere. When he reached the neo-naturalist Anurak Sato, the ship shivered again.

"Interesting. All right, ship. How about *Shikimi Anurak Sato*."

The ship trembled violently but still didn't reveal a door.

"Still not it, but we're close, right?" Marsh dug into Sato's work and found most of it focused on birds and flowers. Particularly one flower with a possible connection. "*Shikimi Anurak Sato Chrysanthemum.*"

A sigh escaped the ship as if it had been holding its breath. Soft crackling followed as a seam began to outline a door on the port side. Marsh held his own breath as he rose, hand still on the ship. The door slid open.

He stood up on the crate and waved both arms over his head until Supervisor Kaneer glanced up and jogged over.

"I can't believe you talked it open."

"Me, either." Marsh gave the ship a side-eye. "Now I'm scared of accidentally saying something that'll trigger it to close again."

Kaneer's eyes widened, then she nodded with a finger to her lips. She jogged off again and returned with a team of silent data techs whom she'd obviously instructed not to speak. Hand signals sent them to different parts of the ship, and Marsh followed them in since she didn't tell him to stay outside.

The inside completely lived up to expectations. Fluid rose-gold surfaces trimmed in soft gray dominated the interior from the cockpit to the living areas at the stern. No boards or controls marred the sleek contours of the cockpit, all the controls most likely contained in the padded chair and on the silvered-out screen taking up the entire nose of the ship. Everything screamed wealth and unearned privilege so loudly that Marsh fought against a niggle of irritation. Different system, different culture—who was he to judge?

Inset drawers and cabinets lined the walls starting

just beyond the cockpit, from tiny cubbies to ones large enough…

Hold on. He approached one of the big drawers near the deck plates, checking and rechecking his readouts. For thirty full seconds, he watched the intermittent blips before he stepped over and pulled on Supervisor Kaneer's sleeve. *Life signs*, he mouthed and pointed to the drawer when he had her attention.

She frowned at the too-slow heartbeat and the heat signature that wasn't nearly warm enough before she sent one of her techs outside to call emergency assistance. The rest of them gathered close as she probed around the drawer until she found the right spot to press. The drawer clicked and slid on silent tracks, cold vapor crawling over its sides as it opened.

The contents had them all staring a bit longer.

A young man lay inside the drawer, so gray-pale he looked like a corpse, and Marsh would've thought just that if he wasn't registering a heartbeat. Thick, black hair lay across his shoulders. He still wore a scarlet flight suit and deck boots that hadn't seen much wear.

He's gorgeous… Marsh couldn't help the thought. Their mystery pilot's face was fairy tale beautiful, even in his unnatural sleep. *Like the prince who slept for hundreds of years. Was it a prince?*

Medics hustling onto the ship interrupted Marsh's drifting thoughts and he had to scramble to get out of the way. After a quick scan and vitals check, the medics bundled the pilot into an isolation gurney, then motioned them all outside.

"Did anyone touch him?" the smaller, older medic asked through their respirator.

"No one got that close," Supervisor Kaneer grumbled. "I don't have time for all these people to go to Decon right now."

"I don't care what you have time for," Older Medic snapped. "We don't know what happened to this young man or why he's in this state. Wrap up and get to Decon. *Now*."

Sighing and grumbling followed the order, but they all knew what they had to do to keep everyone on the station safe. Unknown microbes introduced to the station's closed system could just as easily be catastrophic as they could be harmless, and no stationer would take that kind of chance. Marsh, Supervisor Kaneer, the techs—everyone accepted an isolation suit from the medics and climbed inside them for the short trip to the nearest Medical Aid station. The suits were hot and claustrophobic, and Marsh hated trying to breathe through the filters, but better a few minutes discomfort than putting thousands of people at risk.

From the stuffy heat of the isolation suits to the stinging cold of the sprays in the decon room to shivering while waiting for clothes to pass through the UV cycles, decon always seemed to last longer than its actual twenty minutes. He felt wrung out and done when he finally stepped out again, even though it wasn't even halfway through day shift.

His curiosity wasn't even a little tired, though.

I'll just see where they have him. Maybe come back and check how he's doing tomorrow.

Even as he argued with himself, his feet took him toward the patient rooms, where he started peeking around corners. No one in the first room or the second. The Altairian pilot lay in the third room without an isolation shield, so microbe scans must have been negative. Marsh edged closer, guilt nibbling at him, since he hadn't asked if he could visit. At least the blue tinge had left the mystery pilot's lips and fingernails, his skin closer to golden than gray, though he still lay curled on his side the way he had in the drawer.

Marsh didn't want to be creepy, staring at someone while he slept, but the thick dark lashes held his attention longer than they should have. He jerked back with a squeak when those eyes flew open, his heart hammering from surprise and *not* from guilt over being caught staring. Not at all.

Eyes the color of walnut shifted restlessly and finally focused on Marsh. In a voice no more than a scratchy whisper, the pilot said, "Hello. Where is this?"

It took effort to stop from sinking into those eyes and to formulate an answer. "Um, hey. You're on Bremen Station. They towed your ship in as salvage. Not that it's salvage now. Since they found you, I mean."

"Are you one of Hengist's?"

Those five words shunted Marsh out of his awkward spiral into complete confusion. "What?"

"Did Hengist send you?"

Marsh shook his head. "I have no idea what that means."

"Oh. Oh, good." With that, the pilot closed his eyes and went back to sleep.

That was… different.

Marsh tiptoed out and rechecked his schedule once he got out into the corridor. Problem solved, the pilot seemed to be doing well. Time to move on. Ah. Supply Dock 3–6 had put in a request for him to come look at one of the autoloaders. That might take the rest of the day. Some of those poor loaders were old and not carefully maintained. It had been an unusual morning, but he needed to move on to the next useful thing.

Only… as he skated through the corridors to the Ring Six concourse, he couldn't shake the image of haunted dark eyes.

"WHAT'S YOUR NAME?" The caregiver smiled gently and perched on the end of the bed.

Shiro still wasn't certain he hadn't dreamt the lovely man who had told him he was on Bremen Station. He twisted the blanket between his hands. "I'm not… I don't…" *I'm not sure of anything yet. I don't know whom to trust.*

Her forehead crinkled. "You don't know your name?"

"Pardon?" Shiro shook his head. "Oh. No. That is, I do know my name. I'm uncertain whether I should give it."

"You're safe from any repercussions while you're in Medical." Her voice had grown a hair colder. "Have you done something criminal? Was the ship stolen?"

"Certainly not." He cleared his throat, tamping down hard on his haughty, offended tone. She didn't know since he hadn't told anyone. "No, the ship is mine. Registered to my voice and bio-print. I haven't done anything criminal." *Something that will make my family upset, but I've broken no laws.*

Her expression softened again. "Do you feel unsafe? Is there someone you don't want to find you? Any information you give me won't leave Medical Aid."

You have no idea. He still felt fuzzy and strange after coming out of the hibernation drawer. Next steps, reasonable precautions—nothing made sense. His focus kept returning to whether the gentle-voiced man in the coveralls had been real.

"I'd like to talk to the man who was in here before."

"The medics who brought you in?"

Shiro shook his head carefully so he wouldn't make himself dizzy. "No, I don't think so. He wore coveralls. Umber skin, dark eyes. Short black hair."

"I suppose I can check the feed."

She strode out, and after a few minutes, a whispered consultation happened outside his door from which he couldn't make out much beyond *short, couldn't hurt,* and *doesn't seem comfortable.* Soon the caregiver returned.

"All right, we found your visitor. Marsh Kensinger was the mechanic who figured out how to open your ship. You think you'd feel more comfortable speaking to him?"

There was absolutely no reason he should and yet, talking to Marsh, as brief as it had been, had felt... comfortable. "Yes. Yes, please."

"Very good. You just rest. We've asked Marsh to come by after his shift, which shouldn't be more than two or three hours." She smiled and patted his foot before she dimmed the lights and left him alone again.

He probably should've asked if he could watch a local channel. Three hours without his personal comm, without local nets, without any information at all wasn't going to be conducive to rest at all.

CHAPTER TWO

"And he wants to talk to me?" Marsh shook his head at Donya, the Ring Five psych/social charge nurse. "Why would he want that?"

"Probably something in his background." Donya shrugged one shoulder. "Or maybe—he does have one of those implants. Maybe his ship told him he can trust you."

Marsh gaped at her for a moment. "I don't, um… I don't think the neural-connected ships work like that. And I'm not trained for this. What am I supposed to say?"

"Just have a normal conversation. He seems worried. Possibly even afraid. The way he arrived makes us think he was running or hiding from someone. See if he'll give you his name. Find out if he thinks he's in any immediate danger." Donya turned him and gave him a gentle shove toward the room. "Just talk to him, Marsh. He wants to see you."

But why? I'm just me. Why would he want to see me? Still,

he did as Donya asked and found the pilot sitting up in bed, his thick hair tousled so badly that Marsh had to fight the urge to brush it into place with his fingers.

He gave Marsh a shy smile as he walked in. "Hello again."

"Hi. I'm Marsh. I guess they told you that." Marsh hovered awkwardly halfway between the door and the bed. "You wanted to see me?"

The pilot let out a soft, explosive laugh before he answered. "I wanted to know if you were real." He held up both hands. "I know that sounds silly, but I wasn't entirely awake before."

"You were a little out of it." Marsh waited a beat and finally asked, "So, what's your name?"

The pilot stared at Marsh as if he'd sprouted extra arms. He shook the hair out of his eyes and cocked his head. "Shiro."

"Good. Now I don't have to call you *that pilot* in my head. No last name? Do people from the imperial court not have last names?"

The disbelieving stare lasted longer the second time. Finally, Shiro stammered, "I… ah, I'd rather not say."

"That's okay." Marsh edged closer, rocking from heel to toe. *There's probably some elegant, polite way to ask this, but I don't know it.* "Are you in trouble, Shiro?"

Shiro sighed and stared down at his hands. His posh Altairian accent made his whisper hard to follow. "Am I in trouble? I expect that depends on point of view."

The sorrow running through those words twisted at Marsh's heart. He came to the end of the bed and tried again. "Does someone want to hurt you?"

"Not physically, no. I don't think. Not me, at any rate." Shiro glanced up, an unmistakable plea in his eyes. "Could you find out if certain people are on your station?"

"It's not *my* station… You mean other Altairians?"

"Mostly, yes."

"Did you check arrivals?"

"I'm afraid I don't have any means to do th—" Shiro broke off when Marsh flipped open the wall pad behind his head and pulled up a holo display. "Oh. That's not where I expected a control pad. How embarrassing."

"Different systems than you're used to, I bet." Marsh tapped over to Transit, Customs and Immigration, joining in Shiro's embarrassment when he realized he'd perched next to Shiro on the bed. "Um, right. We've had one Altairian freighter dock in the past week to pick up a shipment. They're already gone. One cutter for a refuel and minor repair, also gone. One ESTO commercial transport, just came in this afternoon."

"That one." Shiro stabbed a finger at the display. "Can we check for a passenger?"

Marsh pulled his hand back from the screen. "It's kinda rude to just go through a ship's manifest without asking."

"Is it less rude to search for a specific person?"

"Who are you looking for?"

Shiro pulled a slow breath in through his straight, perfect nose. "Hengist McClain."

Right. Hengist. That's who he asked about. Marsh threw the search wider than a ship's manifest. "Nothing. No

Hengists on station, and it would stick out. Not a name I've seen before."

"Not one I'd particularly like to see again." Shiro leaned back against the raised head of his bed and closed his eyes. "I realize it's an imposition, but could you check more names for me?"

"Um. This isn't in my usual job description."

"Just three more." Shiro cracked one eye open. "Please?"

Marsh grumbled under his breath, but even just that one eye was too compelling to say no to. "Fine. Three more."

"Touma Saito. Chirag Tazi. Goro Rin."

Who are all these people? Instead of asking, Marsh ran through the searches. "Nothing. None of them is here. Or have been recently."

"Thank you. You're very kind." Shiro seemed to deflate into his pillows.

"You're okay, then? You're safe?"

The little smile that twisted Shiro's lips was anything but happy. "I have some time, at least. Thank you for coming to speak with me. I apologize for taking you away from your day."

Marsh's face heated. He *had* been grumbling about such a simple request and made Shiro feel bad. "No problem. Really. I was done work and I don't do anything after work." *And now I sound pitiful and antisocial.*

He gave Shiro an awkward wave and found Donya at the monitoring desk.

"Thanks, Marsh. Sorry to drag you down here." She looked up from the patient room images with a tired smile.

"I'm sorry. I was really bad at that."

"You were perfect. At least now we know who he is."

Marsh squinted at her. "From just a first name?"

"Don't you watch the interstellar nets?" Donya pulled up footage from a newscast showing the Altairian imperial family at a ceremonial function. She zoomed in on one of the younger people to the left of the empress, and a shock ran through Marsh as he recognized Shiro. Cleaned up and formally dressed, but still. "Our visitor's Prince Shiro Shinohara, one of the empress's kids."

"That's not what I expected." Marsh frowned at the vid, trying not to read into what he saw. Shiro, contained and poised, stood alone toward the back of the royal siblings, not interacting with the others. "Will you tell him you know?"

Donya shook her head. "He's entitled to his privacy. I'll make a note of it, but just in confidential medical files."

"What's going to happen with him now?"

"That's also his business. So many questions, Marsh." Donya patted his shoulder. "We'll keep him here tonight just to make sure his hibernation didn't have any side effects. After that? He can retrieve his ship and go. If he wants to stay, he'll have to go to Immigration for the two-day visitor pass just like anyone else. Beyond that…"

"I think someone's after him," Marsh blurted out. Stupidly obvious.

"From his behavior, he *could* be running from a domestic abuse situation. If he wants asylum, he'll have to apply to Judiciary."

"Just like anyone else," Marsh finished for her.

Donya thanked Marsh again for his help, and he meandered back to his quarters, tired and strangely upset. The moment he stepped through the door, Gally bounced up to scold him in ferret, most likely because he was so late, then bounced back to the food dispenser to request his dinner.

"I'm sorry, Gally. Dinner's probably been warmed up five or six times by now, I guess."

He eased into his single chair to pull off his boots and turn off his limbnet. His legs ached and needed a rest from neuro stimulation. Dinner arrived in a cheerful yellow bowl with green leaves—a bean chili colorado that smelled heavenly but was drier than it should've been, with a red crust around the edge from reheating. Still, he wasn't going to be picky about one of his favorite dinners, and the wonderful taste of mingled smoked chilies was a comfort after a long day.

While he ate, he checked the book club threads. Still no Redmaus. Marsh frowned and checked back through the time stamps. Redmaus hadn't left any comments for several days, which wasn't usual. He hoped everything was all right and found he couldn't start the *Newt's Garden* book without knowing. It just didn't feel right.

Instead, he looked up information on the Altairian imperial family. Empress Himiko—decorated military hero, diplomat, champion fencer—was on her third husband and had twelve children. *Twelve.* Marsh couldn't even imagine it. Crown Princess Masako—decorated fighter pilot, several degrees in various scientific fields, revered poet. Prince Ichiro—decorated fighter pilot, champion swimmer, respected historic translator. Princess Tsuda—decorated fighter pilot, renowned pirate hunter. Cadet Princess Aiko—in pilot training, celebrated for her brave stand against ship hijackers. Prince Hideo—decorated fighter pilot, etc. … *There's a definite pattern here.*

Until he reached Shiro. Prince Shiro—artist. That was the entire entry. Marsh checked other sources, but none of them said much more. A few mentions of *raiwakizashi* competitions, whatever that was. Not yet married. That came up a *lot*. It seemed intrusive to Marsh, but it was probably a big thing for royalty. All the other siblings were married with the exception of Princess Aiko, who probably had to earn her *decorated fighter pilot* byline before she was eligible, and Prince Ren, who was only fifteen.

Shiro, artist. Who stood apart from his family. Who presumably left home alone and put himself in cold storage on his ship. Who had a list of names that made him anxious.

He must have made a sound, since Gally scampered over with grumbling *dook-dook-dook* noises and put a hand on his knee.

"I'm *not* worried or feeling sorry for a prince. That'd be silly, right?"

Chek.

"Not my problem. Not in my skill set."

Though even as he said it, the words settled heavy and wrong in his gut.

IT HAD BEEN AN INTERESTING MORNING. Shiro leaned against the corridor wall, trying to stay out of the way of bots, autocarts, and pedestrian traffic. He stared at the entrance to the salvage bay, unable to come up with a next reasonable action.

He'd gone to Immigration as the nurse? social worker? had suggested, and after explaining several times to several people why he was on the wrong side of the Immigration gate and several calls back and forth to the medical aid station where he'd spent the night, he'd finally received clearance and a visitor's pass.

The next suggestion had been to apply to the Judiciary Board for asylum, though he wasn't at all certain he qualified. None of his pursuers had actually harmed him, though there were others involved who might have been. Shiro reasoned it wouldn't do any harm to speak to the Board, but he was still a mess—unshaven, hair a crow's nest, still in his flight suit. He'd just wanted to get onto his ship to clean up and change and instead had run headfirst into more bureaucracy.

Unauthorized personnel weren't allowed on the salvage bay floor due to safety concerns, and no one on the salvage crews had time that morning to escort him in, so he had no access to either his shower or clean clothes. He apparently could have made an *appointment* with the salvage unit for a supervised escort, but that didn't help him right that moment. He could also have requested to have his ship moved to a regular docking berth, but he would need to pay for a public docking berth, so the location of his ship and the payments would be public record.

Easy to track. Exposing him as surely as if he had

put out a news bulletin with an arrow—*Prince Shiro is here, right here.*

"I didn't think this through very well, did I?"

Several people walking by gave him looks both curious and concerned, but no one stopped. Thank goodness. He didn't need the stationers to think he regularly lurked in shadows muttering to himself.

"Shiro?"

He startled badly, nearly losing his footing as he turned to find Marsh at his elbow. "Oh, hello. Good morning."

"Hi. Are you all right? You look a little…" Marsh waved a hand at him, frowning. The little robotic ferret riding on his shoulder appeared to sniff in his direction. "Should I call you majesty or something?"

"Ah. So you found out." *It was only a matter of time. My face isn't exactly a state secret.* "It would be highness, but no. Shiro's fine. They won't let me to go to my ship."

"Right. No. You're not allowed in there on your own." Marsh twitched and cleared his throat. "But you know that. Um, why did you want to?"

"I just want to clean up and change." Shame flooded Shiro over how his voice trembled. "I wouldn't be in anyone's way."

"You can't—" Marsh actually snapped his jaws shut, frowning harder. *Does he ever smile? It's probably a wonderful smile.* "They want me to go in there and see if I can get the ship's door closed. Why they didn't just ask you… Well, never mind. If you tell me what you need, I can bring it out, and you can use the communal hygiene facilities on this level if you want."

"Communal?"

The discomfort must have been all too clear on Shiro's face. Marsh waved one hand over the other. "*Or* you can use the one in my quarters. I don't mind." He reached up to pet the silver ferret. "Gally will take you and let you in."

"That's very kind of you. Truly." Shiro pulled in a deep breath, trying to draw himself back from the edge of falling apart. "The cabinet above my hibernation drawer has a black bag in it. That has everything I need."

"All right. You'll wait here?"

"I'll wait here." Shiro caught Marsh's arm as he turned to go. "I'm terribly curious. How did you get my *Dahlia* to open?"

Marsh blinked at him, then his confusion cleared. "Oh, the ship. I got lucky. Just started reading Altairian places and names and watched for reactions."

Persistent, more likely. "Lucky or not, I'm impressed." He remembered to let go of Marsh's arm and wanted his warmth back immediately, even though it had been unconscionably rude to grab him. "And thank you. Again."

"Of course." Marsh leaned down to press something on his shoes and *sank* half an inch, and only then did Shiro realize he'd been hovering above the floor. "Want to tell me how to secure your *Dahlia*?"

"Yes. I'm stupidly distracted. Sorry. Just tell the ship, *art critics and gorgons*."

"That's not something I could've ever guessed."

Shiro managed a crooked smile. "Maybe eventually."

Truly pitiful how he reacted to Marsh, since it took

all Shiro's will power not to run after him when he walked away. One friendly face in a crowd of strangers—perhaps in his anxious state that was more than understandable.

THE DAY HADN'T BEEN TOO busy—some work in Salvage, a bit of robotics repair in Culinary—and though Marsh was two hours early getting off shift, he headed straight home to check on his guest. Not that he thought Shiro had gotten lost with Gally to guide him or would damage anything in his quarters. No. This was a more unfocused worry over not being able to name the expression on Shiro's face when Marsh had handed him the bag and given him directions.

Despair didn't seem too far off. Not something Marsh wanted bouncing around in his brain.

When he opened the door, he was relieved to find nothing more dramatic than Shiro kneeling on the floor talking to Gally.

"I don't suppose you also play music—hello, Marsh." Shiro raised his head with a smile, a real one. Apparently, the shower and clean clothes had helped. Instead of the flight suit, Shiro wore a tunic in a soft rose and loose pants in blue, both in a material that had to be natural fiber rather than biopoly.

Marsh resisted putting a hand on his chest as his heart rate returned to normal and likewise resisted blurting out *Good, you're not dead* and *You look amazing.* "Hi. Did you find everything okay?"

"Thank you, yes." Shiro rose, and now Marsh could see his slender feet were bare. Beautiful, perfect feet. "I can't thank you enough for your hospitality. You had no reason to be so kind to me."

"I pulled you out of a refrigerated drawer." Marsh realized he still stood in the doorway and finished coming in so the door could close. "I kind of feel responsible."

"Ah." Shiro sank into the chair by the wall and sat staring at his hands. "I feel I owe you an explanation."

"You don't owe me anything. You're a person and you needed help."

Shiro made a humming sound that could've been a laugh. "You know, I believe you. In a way, it makes me uneasy that you know who I am and have demanded precisely nothing. I'm… not accustomed to that."

"That's horrible." Marsh sat on the bed to face him. "People shouldn't want something from you when you're in trouble."

"I've… read about the Hansa." Shiro finally looked up, his hands curling and uncurling restlessly. "About communal society and the driving attitudes. I just didn't think… well, I thought it must be exaggerated. That there must be grift, selfishness, and corruption just under the surface."

Marsh nodded. "There are selfish people. Of course there are. But no one wants to work with someone like that or have one in their section. If they do something against the codes, there's the Judiciary. If not, they eventually leave. Go somewhere else."

"Social norms to keep the peace. It's an interesting construct." Shiro smiled as he bent to pet Gally's silvery head. His fingers trembled and Marsh pretended not to notice. "It wouldn't work in the empire, but we don't grow up that way."

Marsh slid his hands under his thighs, trying for words that wouldn't be too blunt. "I guess you're more competition driven."

"As a society, I'd say that's true. Competition, merit, obligation." Shiro's hands finally stilled as he clutched the hem of his tunic. "None of that tells you why I was in a drawer in a ship with the engines shut down."

"No. It doesn't. And you still don't have to tell me." Marsh shut up, giving him space. Asking Shiro if he was trying to die probably wouldn't have been the best start. Not that he *wanted* it to be the reason, but it was the reason he dreaded most.

Shiro smoothed his tunic, his gaze returning to his lap as he folded his hands. "I was trying to hide from the men who believe they deserve an answer other than *no* from me."

CHAPTER THREE

Shiro waited three heartbeats, but Marsh said nothing. He risked a glance up and met only concern and confusion in the dark eyes across from him.

"The men after you are sexual predators?"

"Not... no." Shiro let out a hard breath. "I suppose at least two of them could be, though that's not my primary reason. They all believe they were entitled to a *yes* after their *omiai*."

"Isn't that a... a betrothal dinner? Four of them?"

"Welcome to the world of the unattached imperial." Shiro lifted the little robo-ferret into his lap so he would have something to do with his hands. They sat there quite happily making little noises at him. He didn't have to tell any of it. Marsh had said so—twice. But it all began to spill out of him anyway, if for no other reason than he *liked* Marsh. "I suppose an omiai *can* be a betrothal dinner, an acknowledgment. For us, it's the formal introduction to a potential suitor. The imperial nakodo gathers the dossiers of possible suitors. We go through them with Mother and winnow the field down to those acceptable to everyone."

Marsh stared at him, openmouthed. "You're not allowed to marry someone you love?"

"Oh… yes. I'm sorry. I didn't mean to give that impression. Yes, we marry for love, too. My eldest sister has three spouses—the woman and the man she loves, and the woman who was considered the most important political alliance at the time."

"But for you… I still don't understand."

"We're all expected to marry. All of us with a uterus are expected to bear children—"

"Wait." Marsh held both hands up. "Just… hold on. You were forced into a uterine implant?"

The question threw Shiro so badly that he lost his manners and gaped for a moment. "I'm not telling this well. Not at all. No, it's my original one. I was born with a uterus. "

"Crap. I'm so sorry." Now Marsh dropped his head in his hands. "Stupid conclusion to jump to."

Shiro nearly reached across to pat Marsh's knee. "You didn't know. Thank you for wanting to come to my defense, even if the hypothetical offense never occurred. So. Yes. We're expected to form family units. I've never expressed an interest in marrying anyone. Oh, there was a boy at university. I loved him, but he wasn't interested. I've connected with people out on the nets better than I have with anyone in person. Beside the point. As the years went by, Mother became concerned, hence the series of omiai."

"But… four of them?"

"Did I say there were only four? Again, I'm telling this badly. I have had, in the past three years, thirty-five." Shiro cringed as he said it, then hesitated to say more. Marsh seemed to be choking on air.

Marsh got up abruptly and maneuvered around furniture to a wall panel that opened to his touch. "Would you like tea?"

"Yes, please."

Knowing a polite social delay tactic when he saw one, Shiro was content to sit quietly until his host was ready, if he ever would be ready, to hear more. The life of an imperial must have sounded completely insane to someone whose society didn't have hereditary nobility or even a ruling class. He'd heard that many Hansa enclaves encouraged serial commitments rather than lifelong ones. That family units were often fluid and not always genetically related. The freedom to choose or not choose sounded heavenly—no pressure, no expectations. A person attached or didn't without the presumption—the expectation—of future progeny.

Though perhaps there's a good deal of personal instability. Loneliness. Marsh obviously lived alone. Was that by choice?

When Marsh returned to hand Shiro a mug of strong, dark tea and resumed his seat with his own mug, determination had joined the confusion in his expression. "Okay. Let's see if I'm following. You have to get married. By law?"

Shiro sipped, careful not to burn his tongue. "By imperial decree."

"That doesn't sound like a thing you can get out of. And you can marry someone you love, but if that doesn't happen, someone gets picked for you."

"I pick from a field of appropriate candidates, yes."

"But you haven't. You've told them all no."

"So far, that's true." Shiro had to look away from that open, inquisitive gaze, ashamed of his choices, and yet here he was. The backs of his eyes stung as he stared into his tea. "I'd hoped… I'd been so sure that I would sit across from one of the candidates and feel a connection. Something. *Anything*."

"Your mom… Crap. Your mom is the *empress*. That's crazy to think about. Did she pressure you about any of them?"

"Ah. No. Family obligation is pressure of its own, of course. But my mother, my family, they love me. They don't want me miserable."

Marsh leaned forward, mug clutched tight in both hands. "Shiro. Your family's powerful. They would've protected you if one of those suitors threatened you, wouldn't they? Why did you *run*?"

"It wasn't my intention. Hengist… Hengist McClain and the other three names I gave you—all four were insistent. Sending messages, presents, go-betweens, cornering me at public appearances, though Hengist's conversations and messages became more and more distressing. Using possessive language. Telling me I would give in to him one way or another."

"He *messaged* you threats?"

Shiro waggled his free hand back and forth. "Not

directly. Not in any way that I could accuse him of making a threat and be taken seriously."

"If you told them no, why didn't they accept that? And why didn't your mother tell them to leave you alone?"

"I could have gone to Mother. I probably should have. But a grown man running to his mother for help with his suitors is beyond embarrassing. And why they didn't give up is an interesting question. Some men seem to think that continued pestering after a clear *no* is persistence rather than harassment, I suppose. But their specific reasons vary. For the Altairians, Touma and Goro, I represent prestige. Power and influence for families not previously close enough to the throne. For Chirag, I would bring wealth to the marriage. He is a businessman before all else. For Hengist—"

"It's okay, Shiro." Marsh offered softly. "Don't tell me anything you're not comfortable saying."

"Hengist is obsessed. He tells me I'm the most beautiful man he's ever seen. He *must* have me. Things to that effect." Shiro shivered, recalling that hard voice too close beside his ear. "I became exhausted. They wouldn't leave me in peace. I traveled to the family retreat on Ceti Tau, thinking I could find some quiet there."

"Not so peaceful, huh?"

"I've made so many mistakes." Shiro sipped at his now-cooling tea so he wouldn't have to look up. He was an adult and could own his decisions. That didn't mean he wasn't sometimes embarrassed by them. "Mother tells me I'm impulsive. It doesn't feel that way to me. It feels more like panic than impulse most of the time."

"Not everybody's good at split-second decisions. You must've done okay, though. You got here."

"Amazing no one more than myself."

Shiro put his mug down on the shelf beside him and let the story spin out. He had arrived with only his personal guard contingent on Ceti Tau, ready to enjoy the quiet of the lush gardens and the blue-green mineral water pools. For two idyllic days, he did. On the third day, shooting interrupted his breakfast. Sergeant Hana had hustled him to the private hangar, yelling in his ear, *Go, Highness! Get in the air! Get out of the system! We've got your back!*

He'd tried to protest. But skill with the raiwakizashi was useless against distance weapons, and flight was more sensible than forcing his guards to keep him safe in the middle of a firefight. It was the last he'd seen of Sergeant Hana, and his anxiety for his guard attachment hadn't diminished since.

"What if they died getting me out of there? Hana, Jacob, and Yuki and the others. What if they're dead?" Shiro swiped at his eyes, already falling apart during the telling.

"If the Imperial Guards' reputation's true, they found a way." Marsh reached across and took his hand. "You have to hold onto that until you know."

"Yes, of course. Of course." Shiro bent his head to wipe his eyes on his tunic sleeve so he didn't have to pull his hands away. "*Dahlia's* a fast ship. She may not be a Novasym fighter—my reaction times were never fast enough for that—but she was too fast for the ESTO-manufactured clipper waiting in orbit. Hengist's private clipper. One shot from some sort of targeted EM pulse weapon hit, though, and destroyed my communications array."

"He wants you for a husband and he *shot* at you?"

"Nothing hull piercing. Just to disable." Shiro shifted uncomfortably under Marsh's horrified gaze. "Yes, I suppose that still could have gone horribly wrong. But I jumped out-system and tried to get home, or at least to one of the Ceti Prime system outposts."

He'd come out of the short GEM run unable to contact the outposts or pick up any system bulletins. When he spotted two ships blocking his way to the first outpost—not just any ships, but those belonging to Touma Saito and Goro Rin—he began to suspect conspiracies. With no way to call for help or hail the waiting ships regarding their intentions, he'd turned and jumped back out-system.

Eternal system hopping was not a sustainable plan. He'd needed to refuel and had headed for Adanai shipping lanes. The vague feeling of conspiracy cemented when the fourth persistent suitor, Chirag Tazi, found him, still shivering with adrenaline, in the refuel center of an Adanai satellite station.

"He threatened you, too?" Marsh gripped his hands a little tighter.

Shiro nearly said *yes*, then parsed through what had actually been said. "Not threatened. No. He said I looked so lost and alone. That he would protect me. Keep me from harm and distress for the rest of my life. It sounded… At the time, it sounded as if he wanted to keep me locked up somewhere. A man like that—who knows how many people he had watching?

He might have been trying to help, but his words, his expression set off the panic alarms."

"His expression?"

"Hungry. Avaricious. At least, that's what I saw."

Chirag had pointed to a nearby café and said he would wait while Shiro secured his ship. Shiro had agreed with enthusiasm he didn't feel, boarded his ship, signaled the refueling lines to uncouple, and left the station.

"They'd all tracked me somehow, or that's how it felt. I needed a plan rather than simply running again. In hindsight, it was a reckless, ill-conceived plan, but it felt right at the time. I would make certain there were no power signatures, no residual energy readings to track. The hibernation drawer is really for medical emergencies and will keep me alive for a time, even if the ship's life support fails. I jumped into Hansa shipping lanes, shut down the ship's systems, and climbed into the drawer."

Understanding swept over Marsh's face. "And that's why they thought the ship was abandoned. The drawer's so well insulated that no life signs showed on scans. That… was brilliant."

"Up to a point, I suppose." Shiro did take a hand back now to rub his chest. "It was lucky a ship came along to tow me here. I could have been drifting out there for…" He stopped and cleared his throat. "I could still be out there. I might have died."

"You didn't. You're all right." Marsh leaned closer. "Did you get someplace to stay?"

"Oh." Shiro's heart sank into his shoes. Marsh would see him as completely inept. He sailed along confidently enough in his own life… but there were simply things a prince never had to think about. "This is something that, as an adult, I should have seen to. I, ah, I'm not accustomed to being without support staff."

Marsh stood and pulled Shiro up with him. "Come on. Bring your bag. We'll go see my moms at the orchard."

He knew life was different on a Hansa station, but this made Shiro stop in the doorway. "Your mothers live in a tree?"

Marsh was still trying to stifle his snickers when they reached the orchard.

"It wasn't that funny." Shiro side-eyed him, his ears still red.

"Sorry. But it really was."

One side of Shiro's mouth quirked up, so at least he seemed embarrassed and not offended. Wistfulness colored Shiro's voice when he spoke again. "My first visit to a Hansa station, so I'm willing to believe anything. I imagined a giant tree at the heart of the station with apartments built in the branches."

"That sounds beautiful. Like a fairy tale. Did you get to read fairy tales growing up?"

The red deepened to crimson. "Growing up? I still read them."

Marsh bumped shoulders with him. "Me, too. I knew there was a reason I liked you."

There might have been a momentary widening of Shiro's eyes, but it happened so fast Marsh thought he'd imagined it. *At least he's smiling now.*

The scents of sharp citrus and earthy nutrient tanks hit as soon as they'd passed under the archway into the more humid air of the Ring Two orchard. Every second ring had one, larger even than the shipyard hangars in Ring Six, and each grew different trees. Marsh's moms had been the arborists for this orchard—the one with oranges, limes, and mangos—since well before he was born.

The apartment was an odd one, far from the other habitat levels and education pods. No one remembered why this particular orchard had an apartment attached, but it was the oldest part of the station, built before space allocation had been standardized. No family had put in a request for it yet, so Marsh's moms had simply stayed there after he moved out.

"This is beautiful." Shiro stared in obvious wonder and tipped his head back for a deep, satisfied breath. "Wonderful. Gardening in space."

Marsh couldn't help a little tease. "Did you think we'd evolved beyond eating?"

Shiro let out that exhalation sound that was one of his laughs. "No, I thought you must have it all shipped in."

A voice answered from behind the nearest orange tree. "The expense would take the station's entire budget, and the food wouldn't be nearly as fresh."

"Hi, Mama K." Marsh leaned around the trunk to give her a wave.

"Hey, baby boy." She stepped around the tree's elevated tub to give him a one-armed hug since she held pruning shears in the other. "Who's your friend?"

"Keira, really?" Another disbelieving voice came

from a lime tree two rows over. "You don't *know* who that is?"

"I don't watch all the gossip casts like some people, *Dorae*. Don't be rude."

Marsh kept his snicker to a single one. "Hi, Mama D. This is Shiro Shinohara. Really, Prince Shiro. But just Shiro for right now. Shiro, these are my moms, Keira Terrell and Dorae Kensinger."

"So, hon, you going to tell us why you have a prince following you around?"

"*Dorae!*"

"It's all right, Mama K. It's not a usual thing." Marsh rubbed at the increasing ache in his right leg as he told an abbreviated version from finding Shiro in the drawer to how he'd gotten to the station, and ended with, "And if he draws on funds, we're pretty sure at least one of those guys can track him. So I was hoping he could stay with you for a day or two. Since you still have the family apartment."

"Oh." Shiro glanced between them, clearly horrified. "I don't want to impose. We should have called first, at least. I could stay here with the trees?"

Mama D pointed her trowel at Marsh. "His highness has sense. A call first would've been the right thing."

"I know. I'm sorry." Marsh hobbled over to the nearest bench on the path, shooting pains in his left leg joining the bone-deep ache in the right. "Hold on. Just need to turn my legs off for a minute."

Everyone went quiet, and he knew they were watching him. He honestly hadn't meant to make them feel bad, but the limbnet needed to shut *down*. Just for a bit. When he pressed the deactivation and the net released, the relief washed over him sharp and heavy. He gritted his teeth with his head on his knees until he was sure he could look up without tears in his eyes.

"Marsh? What can I do?"

A half turn of his head revealed Shiro kneeling in front of him. *That* was interesting. Also, not *are you okay*, but *what can I do* was doubly interesting. Shiro might've been sheltered. Didn't mean he was selfish or spoiled.

"I just need a minute. It's okay," Marsh mumbled into his knees. "The rig's old and glitchy and needs to reset."

"What does he mean?" Shiro's voice had turned away from him. "What's happening?"

"There was a chemical leak. An industrial disinfectant." Mama K's voice had gone soft and guilty, the way it did when she talked about the accident. "Diluted the right way, it's harmless. But this wasn't."

"It got in the vents. Five people died." Mama D's voice snapped and crackled, hard and brittle. "Keira was pregnant. Wrong place, wrong time. Most of the little ones exposed in utero—they made it, but there were neuro issues the docs couldn't fix."

Marsh pulled in a slow breath and sat up. "My legs and my brain aren't on speaking terms. The limbnet makes that connection."

"But you need a new one. Is it just a matter of funds?" Shiro's forehead had creased in an endearingly worried way.

My prince wants to come to the rescue. The thought started a spot of heat in his chest that spread to his belly. "It doesn't work that way. I'm on the list for one. But people with completely failed ones get them first." *Hold up… he's not* my *prince.*

"I see."

He wanted to erase that disappointed expression from Shiro's face so badly, he nearly reached out to cup his cheek, right there in front of his moms. Instead, he turned the motion into a tug on his own ear. "Sorry. I didn't want to worry everyone. So can Shiro stay?"

Mama K let out a huff. "Of course he can. For tonight. He can't sleep on your floor and he can't sleep in the orchard."

"But tomorrow"—Mama D's trowel tapped his shoulder—"You take a rest day and take his highness to Judiciary to apply for asylum and protection." *Which you should've done already* laced the words so heavily that Marsh winced.

"Yes, ma'am." He reactivated his limbnet and stood carefully, all too aware of Shiro's hand hovering near his elbow. "There. It's fine now. It'll be fine to get home. Shiro, you all right with this?"

"Thank you. Yes." Shiro bowed to Marsh's moms, then straightened, tossing the hair from his eyes as he turned back to Marsh. "I'll see you tomorrow?"

"Right after breakfast." On impulse he leaned forward and wrapped Shiro in a quick, bone-creaking hug. "It'll be okay. You're not alone now."

Shiro nodded as he stepped back, his dark lashes suspiciously wet. They said their good-nights, Marsh got hugs from his moms and an admonishment to call if his rig got worse, and he left the orchard without looking back. Sparks zipped and collided inside him from touching Shiro, and it was a good thing he wasn't staying with Marsh. Somehow, he would've managed to make a fool of himself if Shiro had stayed the night.

He'd almost made it home when one of his search requests pinged.

Immigration registry. 3m ago. Chirag Tazi.

CHAPTER FOUR

The *family apartment* proved to be a good deal larger than Marsh's single-room quarters. A common room and kitchen area led to two separate bedrooms, one obviously meant for a young person with its smaller bed. Even curled up on that too-short bed—and trying his best not to think of Marsh in it—Shiro slept without dreams or waking. That hadn't happened in years.

His anxieties became small, tame things under Keira and Dorae's watchful eyes. They fed him mango slices with soy cream and chili, answered his questions about the trees and the food grown onstation, then sent him to bed. They were so kind, he didn't have the heart to protest being treated like a child, even to himself.

Safe. He felt safe with them. Maybe the perception was a false one, but their apartment beside the orchard seemed a magical place where nothing harmful could enter. All of his anxieties had shifted to the hug Marsh had given him and how Shiro had wanted to melt into his arms or burst into tears or both. Good, strong arms to melt into, and they were nearly the same height, so resting his head on Marsh's shoulder would've been comfortable. So comfortable…

No, no, no, I can't think like that. I have to get home somehow, and Marsh has to stay here. And I've only shown myself to be reckless and scatterbrained in front of him. Why would he be interested in the first place? Of course that spark of interest shows up with a person I can't have. Naturally.

Breakfast was red bean-filled bao and tiny oranges, of which Shiro had three each, carefully watching what his hostesses ate so he didn't take too much. He was debating a fourth bun—they were addictive—when he spotted a box filled with bits of wire and biopoly tubing beside the counter.

"What is all that?" His fingers itched to touch, to sort through for the good pieces.

"Scraps of this and that from the orchard." Keira watched him closely, and Shiro wondered what she saw. "We wait until it's full before taking it to the recycling drawers."

A vague thought that had been rattling around since he woke began to take shape. "May I have some of it?"

Dorae shrugged. "Don't know why you'd want it, but sure."

His fingers led the way as he slid off the kitchen stool onto the floor. "Thank you."

Both of Marsh's moms watched him pull out bits and pieces for a moment, then looked at each other and shrugged. He had something in mind to thank them properly. Hopefully, they'd see it as a thank-you.

"Marsh will be here soon," Keira said gently. "Wait

for him so you don't get lost. We'll be out checking the courtyard trees in Five and Six this morning."

Shiro glanced up, a snarl of wire clutched to his chest. "I'll be here. Thank you for taking in a stranger so readily."

"So polite." Dorae nudged Keira with her elbow. "And they say royals are rude and arrogant."

They set off for work, tool bags slung over their shoulders, and Shiro retreated to the small bedroom with his scavenged pieces to pull his own fine tools from his bag. No soldering, no welding, no gluing today. He'd have to rely entirely on cutting, bending, and twisting.

A latticed wire armature for the base. A sweep of hair-fine blue-green wires for ornamental grass. Red biopoly cut into painstakingly small pieces for petals…

Given their life's work, he was reasonably sure they'd understand.

MARSH HAD CHECKED back along his personal timeline for the past year, then two. No, three. He hadn't taken an unplanned rest day in over three years. With that in mind, he shouldn't have felt guilty about calling in that morning.

He still did.

"Can't be helped, Gally." He booped his ferret friend on the nose, gathered up his pack, and put it back down, reminding himself he didn't need it. "It's not for me, anyway. I have to help Shiro."

Gally gave him an encouraging *chek*, or at least he

imagined it was encouraging, before they climbed up to his shoulder.

"Um, Gally? I'm not going to work today, so I don't need an assistant today."

With a little *dook-dook* and head bob, Gally only clung harder to his ear.

"I see. This isn't about me. You want to see Shiro." He laughed when Gally let out a happy *meep*.

AT LEAST HIS legs didn't hurt that morning, and the limbnet had started up without a hitch. Marsh wished his brain was in such good shape. Dark eyes and amber skin haunted him all the way to his moms' place, and he had to tell the owner of those beautiful eyes something he didn't want to hear.

His heart lurched when he skated through the trees and found the door to the apartment open with no one in sight. "Oh, no."

Had Tazi beat him there somehow? Had he taken Shiro?

"Hello? Anyone home?"

"I'm back here," Shiro called from Marsh's old bedroom.

Marsh tried to get his hammering heart under control as he stuck his head around the corner. "Hey… um. What are you doing?"

"I'm almost finished." Shiro's head jerked up. "Is it all right? Do we have to be somewhere?"

"No rush. Don't worry." Marsh sat on the bed to watch as Shiro fastened little bits of red something to a wire… something. Gally clambered off his shoulder to join Shiro on the floor, nosing at bits and snips. "We don't have an appointment at Judiciary or anything. And it's not far."

Shiro nodded, already immersed in his project again, nimble fingers flying as he assembled the little red-piece-and-wire thing, which soon revealed itself as a flower of many layered petals. He secured the last petal and attached the flowers wire stem to a platform with…

"Oh. It's grass?"

"Yes." Shiro's voice was soft, almost shy, as he finished adjusting the petals. "And a dahlia. A small sculpture for your mothers as a thank-you. Do you think they'll like it?"

"They'll love it. It's beautiful." Marsh helped pick up the leftover bits and pieces. "Is this the kind of art you do usually? Little sculptures?"

Shiro's sigh was barely audible. "I work in a lot of media, but I like this sort of sculpture best—leftover materials, things other people have discarded. It's not considered *real* art, of course."

What? Marsh turned that over a few times and hoped he wouldn't upset Shiro when he asked, "Why not?"

"It's not traditional. Painting, calligraphy, and traditional sculpture are considered dignified, serious art. Fit for a prince or princess to engage in. What I do? The kindhearted art critics call it dabbling. The more conservative ones call it undignified and sometimes monstrous."

Marsh followed Shiro out to the kitchen, where he set the sculpture on the counter, the "grass" swaying gently with every air current. "That's… well, it's stupid. How is one kind of art better than another?"

"If I were someone else..." Shiro's smile had a bitter twist. "It's all right. I'm far enough down the line of succession that my eccentricities are… indulged."

Not an answer. But this was obviously a sore spot for Shiro, and Marsh didn't want to keep digging at it. Besides, he was becoming guilty of putting things off. "Shiro. I have to tell you something you probably don't want to hear."

Shiro straightened, hands clasped politely in front of him. It almost seemed a defensive gesture. "Oh?"

"Chirag Tazi is on station. He arrived last night."

"That was fast." Shiro's shoulders hunched inward. "How do they keep finding me so quickly? They're obviously tracking something other than the *Dahlia's* power signatures. What could they have latched onto?"

"I don't know." Marsh held out a hand. "But we need to get your case filed with Judiciary in case he tries to, I don't know, kidnap you or something."

Marsh's face heated when Shiro took his hand, his body insisting that it craved more contact in ways that might've been embarrassing if he hadn't been wearing loose downtime pants. If Shiro noticed anything, he was too polite or too distracted to mention it.

"Thank you for coming with me." Shiro squeezed Marsh's hand as they closed up the apartment and left the orchard. "Station forms are a little intimidating."

Marsh's heart was still doing cartwheels as they navigated the corridors and Shiro didn't pull his hand away. He glanced down at Shiro's boots, meant for ships and not stations. "I think we better take the tube."

"All right. I assume *the tube* is some species of rapid transit?"

"It is." Marsh tugged him into another turn, the nearest tube access up ahead. "Might be a little weird if you've never been in one, but it's completely safe."

"And somehow, that statement leaves me less rather than more reassured."

"Just stick close." Marsh programmed them for C-8 in Ring Six, then pointed to the doors. "When those open, you step in with me and grab a handle. You can't fall out because of the shields, but you don't want to get knocked around, either."

Shiro made that humming-laugh sound. "Better and better."

Their programmed cube whispered into the loading frame, and the doors hissed open. Shiro balked, and Marsh had to tug him forward into the cube before the doors could close again. Missing the cube wasn't a tragedy, but he didn't want Shiro getting frustrated with the process.

Tube was always a little misleading for nonstationers. The word made them think of simple, linear rail lines of various sorts rather than the three-dimensional, high-speed magnet-driven cubes that rushed about from ring to ring and level to level. The transport system occupied the hollow center of each station segment, connecting every part of a Hansa station like a circulatory system.

"Hold on. Um, to the grab bar, not to me." Marsh wondered if his face was always going to be so hot. He cleared his throat. "Not that I mind, but you'll be steadier."

"Sorry. I'm so sorry."

Shiro's ears were red again, so at least they could die of embarrassment together. Shiro had barely gotten a good grip when the cube *wooshed* forward and he nearly tumbled backward despite his white knuckles on the bar. He might not have had the reaction times necessary to become a decorated fighter pilot, but he had the grace and control to right himself quickly and lean into the acceleration, his lean frame well balanced and strong. Marsh snapped his eyes forward before Shiro caught him staring.

Another cube hurtled directly toward them and Marsh remembered to say, "It's okay. It'll reroute."

Shiro still gasped and squeezed his eyes shut as the other cube leapfrogged over them. He kept his eyes shut until their cube began to ping the destination warning. "What's that?"

"It's telling us we're nearly there. Just be ready to exit when it stops. To your right."

The cube decelerated, stopped, and Shiro staggered out when the doors opened. "That was rather terrifying."

"I should have… you just don't think things are going to be unnerving when you see them every day." Marsh wanted his hand back, but Shiro had tucked both under his armpits. "You're okay?"

"Now that my heart restarted, I'm fine." Shiro gave him one of those bitter smiles. "You must think I'm ridiculous."

Marsh indicated the corridor they needed to follow and got Shiro moving before he answered. "No. I think you're in a place you've never been with things you've never seen."

"You're a lovely person, Marsh Kensinger. I think I

haven't told you that out loud today."

Yep. Permanent heated face. I'm going to be able to cook on my face if this keeps up.

They reached the doors leading to the Judiciary offices just as they opened, and a man stepped out. He stopped, eyes widening, but his gaze went past Marsh to Shiro, who stood frozen two steps back.

The man's eyelids drooped over dark eyes. His smile wasn't anywhere near kind. "Highness. I didn't expect to find you so soon. I've just filed a welfare check request concerning you."

"Chirag," Shiro whispered.

Marsh instinctively moved between them, but the Adanai business tycoon ignored him.

"Just as well. You'll come with me now. Your mother's terribly worried. What were you thinking, running off like that?"

"I'll be in contact with her, thank you." Shiro's hand on Marsh's arm trembled, but his voice remained steady.

"Your actions have been erratic and out of character, highness. Your mother believes you need an escort home." Chirag shook his head, trying to step around Marsh. "I'm sure you won't be able to explain yourself in any sensible way."

"Of course I can." Shiro's grip tightened as his voice rose in pitch and volume. "I needed to get here… because… Because the man I love is here and we wanted to finally be together."

Chirag's eyes narrowed. "This… menial laborer?"

"He's a mechanic. A highly respected one." Shiro slipped an arm around Marsh's waist, pulling him close.

"Shiro, what are you doing?" Marsh whispered in his ear.

"*Please*," Shiro whispered back, a shipyard's worth of desperation in that one word. A black cylinder had appeared in his free hand from… *somewhere*, and its shape set off faint alarms in Marsh's head.

"This is absurd." Chirag waved a hand between them. "How would you ever have met?"

Marsh blurted out, "It was a book club. On the nets."

"Yes." Shiro gave him a quick squeeze. "We like the same sorts of stories and started talking. We've kept it secret since, as you say, many people wouldn't approve."

"But I finally convinced Shiro to come." Marsh knew he was speaking too fast, too loud, but lying tied his stomach in titanium knots.

"You're both terrible liars." Chirag's frown transformed into that terrible, blood-freezing smile. "But go on. Pretend if you like. I'll be here when the ruse falls apart."

"You'll do what you like, I'm sure," Shiro said with a haughty sniff. "If you'll excuse us, please?"

Chirag swept them an ironic bow as he stepped out of the way, and Marsh propelled them through the doors into the Judiciary offices. The black cylinder had vanished again. Not the time to ask about it.

With Shiro still attached to his side, Marsh whispered, "Are you out of your *mind*?"

"I'm sorry. I'm so sorry." Shiro pulled his arm back and ran a hand over his face. "I panicked. It seemed reasonable when I was saying it."

"How could anyone believe that you'd be interested in me?"

"That... *That's* your conclusion in all this? That I couldn't possibly, in any universe, be interested in you?"

Marsh shrugged and shoved his hands in his pockets. "Seems pretty obvious. I'm not rich or nobility or degreed. I've never done anything special. And my legs don't work on their own. Someone who wants to be with an Altairian prince has to be physically perfect, right?"

"You're describing what the imperial nakodo looks for. What the Altairian *media* looks for. What imperial parents have traditionally *looked* for." Shiro's eyes sparked, his words sharp as broken glass. "That's worked so very *well* for me, hasn't it?"

"Shiro, I didn't mean..."

"Never mind. No, I apologize for being sharp with you." The fury in Shiro's eyes faded into brittle weariness. "I'm angry with that... *person*, not you. Insinuating that I'm nothing but a neurotic child. The truth is that, yes, there are historical cases where imperials have made love matches with people who had neither wealth nor status. It's not unheard of."

"Okay."

"You can look it up... Oh." Shiro blinked at him. "You're not humoring me."

"I'm not. I didn't mean..." Marsh sighed. "You're still a prince. I'm still a mechanic. And he didn't believe us, so I don't think he's going away."

Shiro stared past him, arms wrapped tight around Marsh's ribs. For several breaths, he stood there, trembling. Marsh was starting to wonder if he was having a fugue episode when Shiro spoke again. "Marsh. I'm going to ask you something, and if you're not comfortable with it, you must tell me no."

"All right?"

"Would you…" Shiro stopped and swallowed hard. "Would you be my pretend intended for a bit longer? Just until I can get Mother to send people I can trust?"

I'd be willing to do so much more than pretend. But Marsh kept that to himself. "You're really afraid of him, aren't you?"

"Yes. Though I'm far more afraid of Hengist and I know he won't be far behind." Shiro rubbed his hands over his arms. "I know this is an enormous thing to ask. One I've no right to ask. But if—"

"Yes." Marsh held a hand up. *This is a bad idea for me. So bad. But it'll just be a few days. I won't break into pieces when he leaves, since we hardly know each other.* "It's to keep a barrier between you and them. I still feel responsible, you know. Yes."

Shiro turned to stare directly at him. "You will?" Then he flung his arms around Marsh and hugged him hard. "Thank you. You've done so much. I feel terrible asking for more. But thank you."

"It's okay." Marsh hugged him back, telling himself it was just to get Shiro to stop shaking so hard. "I like spending time with you, so it's not like it's a hardship. You ready to go file some cease-contact orders?"

"Is that what we're doing?" Shiro stood back with a shaky laugh. "Yes please, my temporary beloved."

Even though Marsh knew Shiro was teasing, those words threw painful little pins all over his heart.

CHAPTER FIVE

The Judiciary processor had been brusque but not unkind, and Shiro had steadied again throughout the process of filing. She recorded his statements, asked him questions, had him fill out a small legion of forms, and even flagged the cease-contact forms for Hengist as *potentially violent* so Immigration would have alerts for him in the system.

Asylum was an entirely different designation from a visitor's pass, allowing Shiro to stay for a three-month stretch, in which time he could either resolve his issues or apply for a more permanent place onstation. Since he was now listed under Judiciary protection, the *Dahlia* could also be moved out of salvage to a Judiciary-coded berth.

Shiro would have to pay for the docking eventually but had a full year to do so. That was going to be an interesting item to set in front of the imperial bursar.

He held Marsh's hand and leaned against him in relief as they left Judiciary. Pretend, yes. The physical contact was for show, but he couldn't lie to himself and say he hadn't wanted to do exactly this since Marsh had taken him under his steady, competent wing. No. Marsh wasn't a bird. He was a tree, sturdy and sheltering, who had spread his branches over Shiro. Or maybe—

"Shiro?" Laughter danced in Marsh's voice.

"Yes?"

"Are you hungry? I've asked three times, but I think you got lost inside somewhere."

"Sorry. Yes."

Marsh snickered. "Yes, you got lost in your brain, or yes, you're hungry?"

"Both, I think."

"We'll get something in the hub, but first, I want to stop by Clothing Supply for you."

Shiro's eyebrows snapped up toward his hairline. Were his clothing choices so poor? Did they not meet station standards? "I honestly don't need anything."

Marsh pointed to his feet. "Boots. You need mag-levs so you can keep up with me."

Oh, yes. Everywhere around them people traversed the corridors. Some walked, yes, but many, presumably those with farther to go, glided on electromagnetic fields as if they skated on ice. They all wore boots in the same style as Marsh's with the controls near the heel.

"Is it… necessary?" Shiro eyed the skaters with apprehension. None of them struggled, but he had to assume they learned to do this as children. He'd ice-skated once. One disastrous, hip-bruising time.

"I think you might like it better than the tube."

True. "I'll try, but please don't laugh if I make a fool of myself."

Shiro didn't know Marsh well enough to interpret the serious and carefully blank expression. Worry, amusement, irritation—it could have meant any of those or a host of other things. Shiro wished he had his mother's ability to read people, but as with so many other family talents, it eluded him.

Whatever Marsh had actually been thinking, he finally said, "I'll try. But if your falls are spectacular enough, I might not be able to help it."

"It's quite difficult, then?"

Now Marsh gave him a sun-through-clouds smile. "It's not. I'm teasing. And I won't let you fall."

I'm melting. I'm going to melt into an embarrassing puddle of goo in the middle of the corridor, and they'll have to scrape me up into a bucket, and it will cause an interstellar incident. Those bright, beautiful eyes... And now I've done this ridiculous thing where I have to pretend he's mine while pretending that I don't really want him. I'm doomed.

"Thank you. You're very kind."

Perfect. I am also the epitome of bland.

Marsh squeezed his hand and hurried them along. "So what's the last thing you read, since we're supposed to be book friends?"

"It's been a couple of weeks. I'd been hoping..." Yes, reading had been on the agenda for his retreat to Ceti Tau. Marsh didn't need to hear him whine about that. "I think it was *A Compendium of Swallows*?"

Marsh chewed on his lower lip before his expression cleared. "Oh! You mean *A Conflagration of Swallows*? Did you like it?"

"It wasn't my favorite book, no. Too much personal philosophy in lieu of story. Too much *look at all the things I know*."

"Thank stars." Marsh breathed out an exaggerated sigh of relief. "I couldn't get past the first two chapters. I don't mind something deeper, but it wasn't what I was expecting."

Shiro managed a little smile. "Just because it was positioned as historic suspense, you were *expecting* historic suspense?"

"Right? Should've known better."

Warmth spread out from Shiro's heart as Marsh laughed. Even though it was a temporary situation, the light in his dark eyes, his unguarded smile—in that moment, those were just for Shiro. "All right. We agree on what we *don't* like. What was the last book you *did* enjoy?"

The brilliant smile faded as Marsh ducked his head. "You'll probably think it's stupid."

Shiro bumped shoulders with him. "I doubt that since I'll read nearly anything."

"Okay. But a lot of the Altairian critics hated it." Marsh cleared his throat. "It was *The Demon King's New Job*. Based on the fairy-tale character."

"Of course I know that one. Those critics called it frivolous and insulting to a cultural icon." Shiro couldn't maintain a straight face for long. "I loved it. Some critics think they're not allowed to smile."

Marsh put a hand to his chest and let out an exaggerated breath. "For a minute there, I thought you were really offended. You really loved it? I mean, it's silly, but the characters still got under my skin. Sif the Not-Quite Radish is my favorite."

"And that scene in the yogurt shop…"

Before long they were leaning against each other,

snickering helplessly. Stationers stared as they went by, but Shiro surprised himself by not caring.

I've had this conversation before. The thought was so sharp and sudden it made Shiro dizzy. No. It couldn't be.

"Marsh?" he began in a strained voice. "*Do* you belong to a book club?"

"You know, it's a funny thing." Marsh doled his words out slowly as he squinted at Shiro. "On the nets. One of those where everyone uses pseudonyms."

"I… I do, too."

"Shiro." Marsh blinked at him, something like yearning in his eyes. "What's the name of your book club?"

They were both whispering again. "Pan-galactic."

Marsh swallowed audibly and took a hesitant step closer. "*Redmaus*?"

Tears inexplicably prickled the backs of Shiro's eyes. He'd always hoped to meet the person he enjoyed talking to more than anyone else in the galaxy. But this… this was nearly too much. "Stationbookworm?"

"Holy novas." Marsh took him by the shoulders and drew him into a careful hug that tightened when Shiro returned it. "I imagined so many times what it would be like to meet you. It *is* you, isn't it?"

"Yes." Shiro leaned back and managed part of a smile. "Redmaus is me. Stationbookworm once mentioned living on a Hansa station—one of the reasons I headed for Hansa space. But I never thought I'd find *you*, specifically."

Marsh's laugh was unguarded and joyful. "Something familiar your subconscious picked up, I guess. This is amazing. I was worried about Redmaus, about *you*, when you didn't answer my last message. Now I know why."

Nothing had changed, of course. They were both who they had been before with too much separating them, but Shiro's yearning toward Marsh made more sense now. "What did you message about?"

"I saw your comments about *Newt's Garden*." Marsh put a finger to his lips. "Shh. No spoilers. I haven't read it yet."

Shiro took Marsh's hand again and got them moving, a tiny flame holding steady over his heart, knowing that Marsh had worried about him. "All right. *The Demon King*, then. You know there's an entire series?"

"Is there? I hadn't gone back to check."

Shiro allowed himself a tiny moment of smugness. "I could introduce you to the author."

"What?" Marsh stopped again, gaping at him. "You know O. Rin?"

"We've met. At some official function or other." Shiro shrugged. "Royalty has some advantages. Very grandparently sort. They saw me standing by the window and came to talk, claiming they were overwhelmed by all the people."

"You probably know a lot of famous people."

Shiro let out a bare hiss of laughter. "I've been introduced to an absurd number of famous and culturally important people. I don't *know* more than two dozen, and most of those are family."

"Not really happy socializing, huh?"

Nezumi. Hikkomijian. Kamoku. So many words had been whispered when people thought Shiro couldn't hear. Mouse. Awkward. Timid. Not always in a sneering way, but the words were never meant as a compliment. Marsh's question—as shy as Shiro was often accused of being—had been asked without condescension or judgment.

"It's not that I'm particularly anxious about it. I just find it hard to find things to say." Shiro gave a one-shoulder shrug. "I *do* manage to say most of the correct things at social events. But small talk is as draining as being the proper, smoothly polite prince in those situations."

"You haven't had any trouble today." Marsh had that little gleam in his eye again. Was that flirting? Shiro wished he could be sure. It was teasing, at least, which was also wonderful. "Besides, small talk is overrated."

"Entirely."

Shiro's face heated as he said it since Marsh had hit it exactly. Words flowed around Marsh, no effort involved. It was altogether too easy and terribly unfair. This was what Shiro had hoped for, clinging to his pitiful optimism before each and every *omiai*—that *this* one would be different, and a feeling of connection, of ease in someone's presence would finally happen.

The hoped-for spark had never happened until now, with no nakodo or dossier or scheduled *omiai* in sight, with someone he had come to cherish without ever meeting, with someone the imperial court would view as completely unacceptable. Of course. He entertained a daydream where Marsh sat across from him for a formal introduction wearing…something formal. The daydream attire kept shifting between different styles, from formal yukata to military dress to evening silks. They chatted and laughed while his mother beamed at them from the end of the table.

Stop this. This is ridiculous. The whole thing was ridiculous. He needed to secure a hostel room, lock himself in, call home, and wait it out until someone could escort him and the *Dahlia* back home. That was the sensible thing to do rather than entangle Marsh further in an impossible situation.

Except… Hengist hadn't hesitated to attack an armed compound. If Shiro used his funds, his location would light up in red for any scan rat worth their pay. Hengist would probably arrive before Shiro could finish requesting assistance. He would probably attack the station.

All the people living here. Do they even have defenses? I haven't seen a single soldier since I arrived.

No. No, he couldn't put all those lives at risk. His current plan was smarter. Even if Hengist found him, the news that Shiro was already attached would confuse him, buy them some time. This wasn't smart for Shiro on a personal level, but if it prevented violence, so be it.

"Who's your friend, Marsh?"

Shiro rejoined the moment to find he was still clinging to Marsh's hand. They had halted at a counter in a high-ceilinged space, and a woman behind the counter had fastened sharp eyes and a bright smile on him.

Beside him, Marsh stared down at their joined hands as if he'd forgotten about them, then jerked his head up. "Oh. Ah, Ruba, this is Shiro. He's… visiting me for a while."

Those sharp eyes were definitely laughing at them.

"Hello, Shiro from somewhere undisclosed. What can I do for you two today?"

"Apparently, I need a pair of mag-lev boots so I won't slow Marsh down."

Now Ruba did laugh, a sputtering sort of chuckle. "He does fly around the rings like he's on fire some days." Her brow crinkled as she turned back to Marsh. "I can't do a CD-6 for a non-resident on those."

"It's okay." Marsh flapped a hand sideways. "I have credits banked. Lots."

Shiro jerked around in alarm. "Marsh, I can't let you spend your savings on me. That's not right."

Marsh shrugged, a momentary bitter twist to his lips. "Not like I use them for much. At all. Ever…"

Ruba simply nodded to Marsh's muttering, her fingers already flying over the holoscreen above her counter. "That'll do. Shiro, if you could step to your right onto the scanner."

Doing so meant he had to release Marsh's hand, and he missed the warmth encircling his fingers immediately. The muted light of laser measuring moved beneath the scan filters. Not three seconds later, Ruba's workstation beeped in a definitive, smug sort of way.

"There we go. I've got a pair in the back that should fit."

Instead of leaving the counter after that remark, Ruba kept tapping at her screen. Shiro didn't want to be rude, but her behavior puzzled him. Just as he was about to ask about the boots, a knee-high bot on treads whizzed through the door that apparently led to *the back*, a basket clutched in its grab arms.

"Thank you, Rudy." Ruba lifted a pair of boots

from the basket, and Rudy chirped happily at her before whizzing back the way he'd come. "Here you are, young man. There's a chair in the corner if you want to try them on."

The chair wasn't much more than a bent piece of I-beam, but it served. Shiro switched his ship boots for the mag-lev ones, powered them up as he'd seen Marsh do, and stood cautiously with one hand on the back of the chair. *Like standing on a mattress.* He felt steady enough, though, so he let go of the chair and tried a step… and gasped as his feet shot away in opposite directions.

"Whoa!" Marsh's breath hissed as he wrapped both arms around Shiro's waist and kept him from falling. "Don't rush it. Get your balance first."

Shiro blinked, trapped in the mix of amusement and concern in Marsh's lovely dark eyes. "Balance… yes…" Heat flooded his face when he realized he was staring a little too intently. He tried to extricate himself and instead ended up with Marsh's arms tightening when he nearly went over backward. *How can something be so mortifying and so nice at the same time? It's a good thing I'm wearing loose pants.* "I'm terribly sorry."

"You've got it." Marsh eased back, hands still on Shiro's hips as if they were dancing. The tops of Marsh's ears had gone red and he swallowed hard. "Don't, um, let the cushy feeling throw you. They're still your feet. You're still in control."

I'm embarrassing him. This won't do. I can manage this. He tightened his core as he would for any other balance-reliant move and shuffled his feet experimentally. Good. Yes. Something like ice but more forgiving. Just enough give to make movement possible. Not *walking*, but the skater's glide Shiro had witnessed many times now onstation.

He kept hold of one of Marsh's hands and pushed off his right boot to glide forward half a meter. Then the left. He kept one hand on Marsh and skated a circle around him.

Marsh gave him a soft hint of a smile when he glided back around. "You've got it. Now let go."

With a sharp breath and a little stumble, Shiro did. The illusion of a cushion under his feet evolved into a sensation of skimming across fog, as if he no longer had substance and skated above the ground as a restless ghost. He did his best to set morbid thoughts aside as he glided past Marsh again, whose eyes followed him with keen concentration.

"I think I have it," Shiro said on his next short run past. "Now how do I stop?"

To Shiro's relief, that proved to be easier than finding his mag-lev balance. He simply had to tilt his foot and tap a toe on the floor to stop the glide. Marsh laughed when he managed to stop smoothly, a warm sound that wasn't derisive or mean-spirited. It was delighted.

"There. He's all set." Ruba shooed them with both hands. "Now get out of here before all the smoldering looks set my depot on fire."

Smoldering…?

"Um, right." Marsh's smile had vanished, his gaze glued to the floor. "Thanks, Ruba. We should… lunch. Yes. Lunch."

He powered up his boots, snagged Shiro's sleeve and propelled them both out of Clothing Supply. Shiro kept up after an initial stumble, frantically trying to parse Marsh's expression. Was he angry? Annoyed? Frustrated?

Finally, he slowed so they could glide side by side along a wide corridor. He glanced sideways at Shiro. "I'm so sorry. I hope she didn't embarrass you too much."

Ah. Mortified.

Misery tinged Marsh's voice and Shiro scrambled for words to make him feel better. He wasn't good at this. Mother would have known with hardly a thought. After agonizing for a few moments, though, it hit him that Marsh was upset because he thought *Shiro* had been humiliated.

"Not at all." He squeezed Marsh's hand and shot him a quick smile before he had to concentrate on where his feet were again. "We're pretending we're together, so we must be doing something right."

He got the laugh he'd hoped for, but unlike Marsh's earlier laugh, this had a sharper edge. Not a happy laugh, not entirely. Then Marsh's gaze grew distant, and his voice was soft again when he spoke. "It's like we're naturals at it."

Shiro managed a smile, though he couldn't find words to answer that. *Naturals. Yes.* If he thought about that too much, he'd just get depressed.

They skated through the corridors, Marsh tugging at his sleeve from time to time to correct his course or to pull him out of the path of oncoming traffic. In a hallway full of little food shops that Marsh called Concourse Five-Six they had bao, and Shiro asked, half to himself, about where the station got the rice flour. The bao vendor was pleased to tell him all about the high-yield hydroponic rice specifically modified for station growing.

"Thank you," Shiro murmured after the explanation. "So much I don't know. Are the stations entirely self-contained?"

Marsh and the bao vendor shared a chuckle before Marsh shook his head. "We don't have everything. Not like the station's magic or something. Lots of grains. Textiles. Fruits that don't grow well onstation, like cranberries. Those get imported. But they're not cheap."

"Of course, of course." Shiro tapped the tips of his forefingers together, thinking, and twitched when he realized the vendor was staring. "Ah. Thank you. For indulging my questions. It's my first time on such an enormous station."

"Come on." Marsh tugged on his sleeve again. "I want to show you something."

Shiro gave in willingly and resolved to stop creating situations where Marsh thought he had to rescue him from embarrassment. Marsh mentioned another concourse, which by now Shiro understood was the connecting corridor between one of the station's gigantic, multilevel rings and the next. As they cleared the arch exiting Ring Four, he understood immediately why they'd come.

Instead of the metal-and-ceramic walls of the other concourses, this one was a clear cylinder with an unobstructed view of the stars all around, giving the illusion that the walkway floated in space.

"This probably isn't such a big deal for you." The vast dark surrounding them nearly swallowed Marsh's soft voice. "You've probably been out in the black hundreds of times. For me… I like coming here. Pretending I'm out there, flying somewhere new."

Shiro shook his head, taking a moment to catch his breath. "No, it's beautiful. Amazing. I might fly, but I've never *walked* among the stars." The rest of what Marsh had said caught up a moment later, a strange spark of hope firing in Shiro's heart. "You want to leave here?"

"It's just a daydream." Marsh stopped halfway across, gazing out at the galaxy. "I'd like to see other places someday, sure. But this is home."

"Of course. There's nothing like coming home."

Shiro stepped behind him and wrapped both arms around Marsh, resting his chin on Marsh's shoulder. Gratitude swamped him when Marsh leaned back against him with a soft sigh, and there, with Marsh in his arms and the stars surrounding them, the sensation of his heart quietly breaking seemed a distant, indeterminate thing.

CHAPTER SIX

When Shiro mentioned how he'd been thinking of getting a hostel room, Marsh shook his head. "We better run that by my moms first. I don't want to get caught in the crossfire if you just pack up and go."

"I'm not certain it matters any more if I use funds, since Chirag's already found me."

"Believe me, that's only half the problem."

Shiro threw up his hands in an uncharacteristic gesture of frustration. "But I'm clearly imposing. I can't keep inflicting myself on your mothers like a… a *leech*. And—"

"I hear you, but maybe let them decide that." Marsh kept them moving forward, back to his mothers' apartment. "Or I'll be hearing about it for the next three years."

They'd almost made it when they were ambushed in the orchard.

"*You* made the dahlia sculpture?" Mama D pinned Shiro with a glower.

Shiro gave ground and swallowed hard. "I… yes? Did I… is something wrong?"

Mama K's hands flew to her mouth. "We thought you were just a *prince*."

"I'm very confused." Marsh glanced between moms and Shiro. "You're annoyed that he made you a sculpture or that he's an artist or what's going on here?"

"Not annoyed about the sculpture," Mama D grumbled. "Just caught off guard."

Mama K flapped her hands at them. "And feeling silly that we didn't make the connection until we saw Shiro's dahlia. *That* artist."

"Nope. That didn't clear up anything." Marsh stuffed his hands in his pockets. "Still confused."

Mama D pointed to the apartment door and waited to start explanations until they'd all trooped inside. "You remember the last remote exhibition your mama and I went to?"

"Um, no? You go to a lot of them." Marsh took a seat at the counter, since his legs were starting to twinge. "I only remember the ones when I've gone with you."

"He can't remember all of them, Dorae." Mama K got out mugs for tea. "Marsh has a life. Anyway, the last one we went to was an *ikebana kinzoku* exhibition featuring an artist who only called themself Gorgon. All inorganic material, but such, oh, *exquisite* floral arrangements. We were both just stunned."

"And then we come home and find this…" Mama D pointed to Shiro's little sculpture. "A piece that looks an awful lot like those pieces made from the bits we both saw a certain prince take out of our scrap bin this morning."

Shiro hadn't quite hunched, but his eyes were on his hands in his lap, and he looked like he wanted to melt into the furniture. "I apologize. No deception was meant. I... sometimes I exhibit under Gorgon so the critics will see the pieces and not the imperial hands that made them. I've caused offense and I do apologize for imposing. I'll get my things—"

"You'll sit your imperial butt back on that stool is what you'll do, your highness," Mama D said in her most intimidating voice. Shiro sat. She ran both hands back over her braids. "You haven't offended us. Yet. But you leave us a little thank-you gift that's probably worth more than our food allowance for a year and we're gonna be a little—we can't accept something so valuable."

"Oh. I see." Shiro still hadn't looked up.

"Moms." Marsh put a hand on his shoulder, squeezing gently. "Don't do that to Shiro. What's he supposed to say to that? Systems away from home, with no access to his ship, he gave you what he could. Something he thought you'd like. And if no one but us sees it, the only value's in the thank-you, isn't it?"

Shiro's eyes shone as he looked up at Marsh. "I should still go. What if I'm putting your family in danger?"

"What? No, no, no." Mama K flapped both hands at them. "Absolutely not. You're safer here than you would be in any of the hostels near the hangars. No. We won't hear another word." She stepped forward, took Shiro's hands, and glared at Mama D. "And don't mind us. We were a little shocked when we put things together. That's all. It's a beautiful present. Thank you."

"Yeah. Okay. Sorry, kid," Mama D muttered. "That's what I meant."

Shiro looked ready to protest again, so Marsh headed him off. "They're right. You're safer sleeping here. Farther from Immigration in a place where outsiders aren't likely to look. If they look at station schematics, this area just comes up as *orchard*."

"I suppose that's only sense." Shiro spread his hands. "But I am sorry I've involved all of you in this."

"That's it. I've hit my apology quota for the week. Dinnertime." Mama D leveled a finger at Marsh. "You're staying, baby boy."

"Not gonna pretend I'm sad about that." Marsh gave Shiro a reassuring squeeze and settled back on his own stool. "That's the second time gorgon's come up. Now you have to explain."

Shiro's eyebrows crept upward. "I do?"

"Hey, I don't make the rules."

Finally, Shiro's expression eased away from stricken to almost amused. "I see. There's nothing complicated or sinister about it. My first public display was a larger set of sculptures in a park. They were meant to be gorgons— Medusa and her sisters. They weren't well received, but no critic will openly criticize a member of the imperial family. They called the installation things like *novel* and *a vision of apocalyptic plant life* and *an interesting first effort*."

Marsh shook his head. "Wow. How to be mean and still be polite."

"Passive-aggressive nonsense." Mama K *tsked*. "If you can't say what you mean, don't say anything."

"I appreciate the support. I was only fifteen and my craft has improved a bit since." Now Shiro did manage part of a smile. "But in honor of that shaky start, I use the name Gorgon when I want to show anonymously. I save exhibiting under my own name for charity events."

"And you show anonymously so you can get an honest read on your work." Mama D plunked a plate of sliced mango between them.

When Shiro didn't take a slice, Marsh acted on a hunch and took one first. Yep. Then Shiro took one. Polite was so well ingrained that it never cracked.

"Yes. Oddly, when Gorgon does experimental work, something more like my first installation, the critics are far less condescending." Shiro shook his head with one of those hum laughs. "I feel as if that should point to something profound, but I've no idea what."

Dinner joined the mango on the counter within a few minutes, something easy, quick, and one of Marsh's favorite comfort foods—potato pancakes with applesauce. Good, simple food. Maybe too simple for Shiro. Marsh snuck a side glance, but no, Shiro's eyes shone as he took exacting, polite bites of pancake, clearly relishing every bite. Appreciating it just as he had every other food offered to him.

He couldn't decide yet whether Shiro enjoyed their food as a novelty or if he was incredibly easy to please. Maybe both.

"When you think about it…" Marsh spoke into the contented eating silence. "Your work and my work aren't really that different."

Shiro blinked at him. "I'm sure you had to train for years to do what you do."

"And I bet you weren't born making art." Marsh bumped shoulders with him. "I meant the physical parts of it. Soldering, welding, wrangling wires and chips, handling tools from tiny pliers to overpowered riveters."

"Ah. Yes, that's true." Shiro gave him a tiny hint of a smile. "Though your skills keep vital systems running and mine only annoy art critics."

As he laughed, Marsh was aware of his moms watching them like security bots, but only on the edges of his concentration. Most of his attention was on that smile, the one that peeked out more frequently the more time they spent together, and the way it transformed Shiro's face from somber-handsome to achingly beautiful. But the smile vanished as quickly as it appeared.

After frowning at his empty plate a moment, Shiro said, "I have to get a message through to my mother somehow. I'd normally do that from my ship, but the comm's damaged."

"We don't have long-range here." Mama D pointed stationward. "But Marsh could take you to the central comm office tomorrow."

Shiro twitched. If Marsh hadn't known what to look for by now, he would've missed it. The minute tightening of his hand. The little tic at the corner of his left eye. "I can't disrupt your work schedule again. I'm sure I'll find it with some directory help."

Guilty for being a burden and always trying to take up less space. That much Marsh had seen in a short space of time. "I'll come get you before. It's no problem getting you there and introducing you. That way you won't have to waste time explaining who you are and why you should get access." Marsh put a hand on his arm when Shiro stared at the counter without answering. "You with me?"

"I'm here. Sorry." Shiro let out a strangled sound that might have been a laugh. "Yes. Thank you."

By the end of dinner, Mama K had convinced Shiro to stay with them. If Marsh had to guess, he'd say that Shiro's acquiescence was as much relief as it was careful politeness. He nearly gave Shiro a kiss on his way out, remembered that they hadn't shared the pretend relationships with his moms, and settled for a quick, reassuring hug.

He whistled most of the way back to his quarters, a warm glowing crucible taking up most of the empty space inside him. The more he tried to ignore it, the more the stupid thing insisted on glowing.

SHIRO KNEW he was skating fast enough to risk overbalancing, but his anger needed to go somewhere. Trying to push it out through his feet seemed more reasonable to him than punching the nearest wall.

Someone was blocking the signal to Ceti Prime.

The tech at the comm center had been baffled and had tried everything she could, but she couldn't get through. Not on planetary channels. Not on military channels. Not on his mother's private channel, which should have been foolproof. All the techs at the comm center consulted and yes, it wasn't just outgoing. There had been no signals coming in from the Altairian homeworld that morning—no messages, no shipping requests, no newscasts. The tech promised to get more hands on the problem and root out the source, which Shiro appreciated. But that someone had gone to such trouble…

It frightened him, and the fear had brought on an unaccustomed bout of fury. Shiro had managed to remain polite as he left the comm center. Yes, he appreciated their efforts. Of course, yes, he understood it was unprecedented. Who to contact if they had news? Marsh? Yes, thank you.

This conspiracy. Coming after him in his family's sanctuary. Blockading his path home. Tracking him across the galaxy. Disrupting communication with his mother. How *dare* this batch of—

"Prince Shiro!"

The shout felt like a fist to the heart. Shiro couldn't immediately recognize the voice, so he kept skating down the concourse, neither slowing nor turning.

"Prince Shiro!"

Running footsteps pounded after him, curses and shouts echoing through the crowded concourse. Reluctantly, Shiro slowed and stopped rather than endangering station residents, since his pursuer apparently had no issue plowing over people. He pulled in a slow breath, gathering his calm and his royal mask before he turned.

While he wasn't shocked to discover who was behind him, the betrayal still stung. He mixed ice shards with his words as the man skidded to a stop in front of him. "Goro Rin."

"Highness! Thank goddesses you're all right!" Goro puffed, hand on his chest. An old war injury might have been troubling him. Shiro did his best not to feel bad about that. "Where is your guard, my prince? Why are you alone?"

Shiro fought the urge to back away and drew himself up to his not-considerable height. He couldn't show nerves or fear. "Don't pretend you don't know. You and your little cabal. After you block my way home? After you somehow cut communications through imperial channels?"

"Highness…" Goro's eyes had grown huge. If he was acting, Shiro had to concede it was convincing. Slowly, he sank to his knees. "Prince Shiro, I have spent my life in Her Imperial Majesty's service. I am loyal, as I have ever been."

"Then why are you here?" Shiro's jaw was so tight it ached, his voice threatening to crack. "Why did you follow me?"

"Your mother received intelligence concerning the attack on Ceti Tau." Goro spread his hands, coming up to one knee. Pedestrians were stopping to stare. "Your last confirmed location at an Adanai station concerned her greatly. She has sent envoys to hunt down information and I was dispatched to follow rumors of your presence here."

Shiro closed his eyes and let out a slow breath. "Get up. Please. You're causing a scene."

"Apologies, highness." Goro had to put a hand on the wall to stand again. "Your beauty overwhelms good sense."

I did almost feel bad. Almost. "If you are loyal." Shiro held up a hand to stop the immediate protestations and put it right back down to hide his shaking. "And if you had nothing to do with the attack or the way I've been stalked, you will discover who has blocked the comm channels and why."

"As you command." Goro bowed, crisp and formal. "You know I would die for you."

"I'd rather no one did, thank you."

Goro took that as a dismissal, bowed again, and stalked off, perhaps offended, perhaps angry on Shiro's behalf. His mother would've handled that better, would've managed to make it clear she wasn't interested and still made sure that Goro felt appreciated. Respected. Of all the persistent suitors, Goro Rin at least deserved the respect due a war hero.

Shiro shook his head and resumed his progress down the concourse at a slower pace. He wanted to return to the relative safety of the orchard for a few hours and think in peace for a bit before he found his way back to Ring Five to meet Marsh for lunch. Two cross corridors on, he realized he should have asked Goro about Sergeant Hana and the guard attachment he'd had with him on Ceti Tau. *Stupid, stupid, so stupid.*

Maybe by the time he saw Marsh, his shaking would be back under control. Shiro wanted very much for Marsh to see him as other than a complete mess that day.

MARSH RACED DOWN THE CORRIDORS, dodging and swerving around slower pedestrians. There probably wasn't any reason for panic. Probably. But he'd promised to keep Shiro updated, and Marsh's head had been stuck in an evaporator unit with a glitchy dampener field.

The alert that Goro Rin was on station had come through almost half an hour before he'd seen it.

He's sensible. He'll be all right and stay where people can watch out for him. He's a grown person. Managed all these years without you.

But I worry. It's my best thing.

No helping that. Shiro hadn't said much about Goro Rin—whether he was violent or dangerous in some way. With his other morning work assignment moved to that afternoon, Marsh raced off to find Shiro. He hadn't been at the comm center, though Marsh hadn't expected him to be there still. But he hadn't been at Marsh's moms, either, which was more worrisome. Marsh's next thought was that restlessness had driven Shiro from the apartment and out of the orchard. They'd agreed on a spot for lunch, and maybe Shiro had just gone a little early.

Gally squeaked from Marsh's shoulder as he rounded a corner too fast, but he couldn't stop now to reassure his AI companion. Relief hit him so hard he stumbled when he spotted Shiro sitting on the bench in the middle of the Three-Four Concourse, staring out at the stars. He caught himself on the railing and slowed his glide for a graceful stop in front of Shiro.

"Oh. Hello." Shiro blinked up at him, a slow smile blossoming on his face. "You're early."

Marsh bent over his knees, still breathing hard. "Had an alert. Immigration. Goro Rin."

"Hmm. Yes." Shiro's gaze wandered back to the stars. "I spoke to him."

"You..." Marsh plunked onto the bench beside him. "Are you all right?"

Shiro grimaced. "I handled it badly and I'm

ashamed for that. No, I'm fine. He didn't… He *might* actually be here on behalf of my mother."

"But you're not sure."

"I'm not sure." Shiro heaved a whispered sigh. "I was… I wasn't gracious. He walked away before I thought to ask him things I should've asked. I'm worried for my marines, but I was too startled by having him pop up in front of me to ask if he had news."

Marsh reached for his hand, almost without thinking it had become that natural. "But you don't feel like he's a danger to you?"

"Not… well, not immediately, at any rate."

After sliding from Marsh's shoulder, Gally booped their nose against Shiro's arm. Then they slipped to the floor to explore under the bench with occasional *dook-dook* sounds.

Marsh took his hand back to unpack lunch from his bag—oranges today, and white-bean-and-vegetable soup. Yes, food for two was over his usual allotment, and he had to spend the extra credits. But as he'd said the day before, he had a ton of credits banked and for Shiro, he certainly didn't mind. That hint of a smile when Shiro opened the container and breathed in the steam? More than worth it.

"So we have Chirag, who's waiting to see our relationship fail or be exposed." Marsh took a bite of soup without thinking. "Ow. Hot, hot. Anyway, not a real threat since he doesn't seem willing to do something illegal where people are watching. Probably. And Goro, who may not be a threat at all. Possibly."

"So far." Shiro took a more careful bite. "Touma I

just don't know well enough, but I won't be shocked to see him pop up here. It's Hengist..."

"Right. He's the one to worry about. But he's not here."

A shudder ran through Shiro and for a moment he sat frozen. Finally, he whispered, "He's coming. I can almost feel it. Somehow...he's done something or Chirag has done something. Maybe they worked on it together, to make me trackable."

"They won't let him onstation. And they won't allow him to dock with armaments." Marsh leaned his head against Shiro's shoulder. "He can't get to you here. This is Hansa space."

Shiro's whisper was so spare, even right beside him Marsh thought he might have imagined it. "I thought imperial space was safe, too."

"Prince Shiro!" a well-projected tenor called from the end of the concourse.

Marsh leaned around Shiro, spotting a man in a bright-blue cat suit and impractically heeled boots trotting toward them. Three large men carrying a variety of heavy equipment followed him.

"Oh great. A news model. Do you want to outrun them?"

"No." Shiro sat back, regal and seemingly at ease, and took Marsh's hand. "They just find you again. It's all right. *This* I know how to do. Look at the interviewer, not the imagers. I have the feeling Chirag called the press about our engagement."

"But... broadcasting your location?"

"It's already too late."

Shiro flicked a glance toward the opposite

entrance to the concourse where Chirag leaned against the wall. The bastard definitely had set this up.

"Prince Shiro!" The news model's smile threatened to swallow the entire concourse. "Do you have a moment to chat with us?"

Shiro had pulled out a bright smile from somewhere. It didn't look natural on him. "Hello, Sasha. It's nice to see you again. Of course I have a few minutes."

The news model—Sasha Benitsky no less, not just *any* news model—preened and fixed his already perfect hair, obviously pleased that Shiro remembered him. "Thank you, highness. We've heard from an anonymous source that you might be recently *attached*. Would you care to comment on that?"

"Certainly." Shiro raised Marsh's hand to kiss the backs of his fingers. "This is Marsh, my fiancé."

The smile had turned slightly predatory as Sasha's attention swiveled. "Marsh Kensinger, I understand you're a mechanic."

Just a mechanic was too evident in that statement. "I'm a union-licensed utility mechanic. The only one on Bremen Station."

Sasha turned, all business and sharp gestures, to the bruiser overloaded with holo imager gear. "Mark that, Charlie. I might have follow-up later." The smile reasserted itself as he swiveled back. "Highness, I understand you met through a book club?"

"We did," Shiro answered, calm and pleasant.

Sasha's smile took on a coaxing, you-can-trust-me veneer. "I'm sure our viewers are just dying to know which one."

"I can't divulge that, I'm sorry." Shiro shook his

head as if he actually were sorry. "The other members deserve their privacy."

"Of course, of course. Did the other members know who you are?"

Marsh squeezed Shiro's hand and picked up the thread. No need to make Shiro do all the work. "Everyone joins under pseudonyms. It keeps the conversation unbiased."

"We liked the same books." Shiro slid him a conspiratorial side-eye. "And disliked the same books. And very much enjoyed discussing them."

One of the bruisers had produced a folding chair for Sasha so he could sit half-facing them. "Would you like to share which ones?"

"I'm so sorry, Sasha, but no." Shiro still smiled, but his eyebrows drew together to indicate gravity. "That would be an endorsement, which must be handled through channels."

"Apologies, highness. But this all sounds so romantic! You didn't even know each other's names."

Marsh leaned into Shiro. "We didn't. Not at first."

"Were you shocked, Marsh? When you found out the man you were falling in love with was an actual prince?"

"Sure. Of course. Not something you really think about, right? But Shiro's so kind and grounded. He's talented and smart and funny. Who we are was more important than *what* we are."

Sasha asked a few more fluffy questions, then snapped his fingers to have one of his crew come forward with a tablet to sign releases. Finally, he stood and offered Shiro a graceful bow. "Thank you, highness. The exclusive means so much to the network."

"Certainly." Shiro gave a regal nod. "Though I wonder if you'd do me a favor."

"I'm intrigued." Sasha posed with a hand on his chest. "Do go on, highness."

"Could you make certain this goes out on the Altairian nets?"

Sasha's expression turned sly. "Haven't told your imperial mother yet?"

"I haven't been able to." Shiro's expression had turned to stone. Angry, Marsh thought, but too civilized to raise his voice. "Someone has constructed a communication blockade between the station and Altairian space."

"There's a lot more to this than either of you are saying." The wheels spinning behind Sasha's eyes were almost audible. "I'll take the broadcast far enough out of station range until I can make certain it reaches Ceti Prime if you promise me an exclusive when this is over."

"All the details, Sasha. We'll speak to no one else."

Marsh stayed quiet until Sasha and his crew of silent giants were out of sight. Vain and a little shallow, maybe, but that one was sharp as shattered glass. He finally said to Shiro, "That was clever of you. But Chirag had to know the story would get out."

Shiro drummed his fingers on the bench. "I think he was counting on it. Wanting my mother to come storming in here and forbid our relationship."

"And you just want your mom to know where you are and that you're okay."

"I do." Shiro turned to face Marsh, capturing both

his hands. The tops of his ears pinked, and he swallowed hard before saying, "There are a lot of things I wish hadn't happened. But meeting you isn't one of those things."

"I… Shiro…" *I think you're great. I'm glad we met, too. I desperately wish you could stay.*

Marsh didn't manage to say any of those things as Shiro put a hand to the side of his face, leaning in slowly, deliberately, giving him a chance to pull away. Words were a thing. He'd forgotten how they worked as he grabbed a fistful of Shiro's shirtfront and pulled him closer. Shiro slid his hand to the back of Marsh's neck as their lips met, softly, oh so softly in a tentative dance of request and permission.

A low, desperate sound rumbled in Shiro's throat and he lunged forward, pressing against Marsh as if he couldn't get enough contact, his lips demanding and suddenly everywhere—along Marsh's jaw, down his throat, sucking on the bit of exposed collarbone.

"*Shiro*… gods…"

They were in the middle of the concourse. Anyone could see. Marsh needed to back away, remind Shiro of… of something… Instead Marsh squirmed as Shiro slid his hand down to his hip. His knee brushed against the lunch set out beside him. An orange rolled off the bench.

Shiro's free hand shot out and grabbed it before it hit the floor.

Breathing hard, they both stared at the bright globe.

"I thought you said your reflexes weren't good enough to be a pilot," Marsh whispered.

Shiro handed the orange over with a shrug.

"They're not. Or rather, different sort of multi-input ones. Our reflexes are trained from birth. Some of it simply didn't take with me."

"Got it. Making a note not to make anyone in your family mad at me."

If Shiro's humming laugh vibrated into Marsh's core, well, he'd just have to ignore that like he did the ache in his chest that just wouldn't go away.

CHAPTER SEVEN

"**A**re all residents station-born?" Shiro asked the question with half his concentration. The other half was busy fixating on the glove Keira had given him. The material on the palm turned red if he touched a ripe lime and remained an inert beige if the lime wasn't ready for picking.

"Most are." Dorae grunted as she shoved the hover-bin closer to them. "Not everyone, though. There's standards, but people do immigrate and apply for residence."

Bees made of light had invaded his head—an entire hive. They'd zipped around Shiro's brain in distracting ways ever since he'd kissed Marsh. Staying on one thought for more than a glimpse at it had become difficult. The bees were flame, sending warmth through him. No, they were glass and flashed mirrored reflections and prismatic rainbows. No, they were velvet, soft and insulating, filling up the empty spaces—

"Shiro?" Keira stood at the foot of his ladder.

"They're very pretty limes, but they need to go in the bin."

"Oh. Yes." Shiro felt his face warm when he realized he'd been staring at the same lime for goddess knew how long and dropped the ripe fruit into the harvesting bin. Navigating his way through his head bees, he managed to locate the last thing Dorae had said. "I imagine immigrants are people with special skills?"

Dorae harrumphed. "Some kind of skill, anyway. We don't have the space for royalty to be lounging around everywhere."

Keira hissed in a sharp breath. "Do*rae*."

"What? *He's* not loafing." Dorae pointed pruning shears toward Shiro. "And besides, he has actual skills, if it came to that. Fine tools and such."

Keira still shook her head. "But yes, an outsider has to be able to demonstrate that they'll be beneficial to the community. And they'd have to be able to join a union, like everyone else."

"Are there..." Shiro hesitated, locating another ripe lime before he went on. "Are there many unions? Every job has one?"

"Probably not as many as you'd think. We're Growers Union, but that includes everyone involved in making food, even the lab folks who synthesize proteins."

Shiro tried to guess. "And Marsh is Mechanics and Engineers Union?"

"Almost." Dorae hooked the bin and pulled it to the next tree, the signal that Shiro should follow with his ladder. "Marsh is UEAMM. United Engineers, Artificers, Mechanics, and Machinists."

"Bit of a mouthful."

Keira's too-serious face might have been holding back a smile. "We would never tease him that they have to adjourn meetings once they get through the name."

"Never," Dorae added, equally solemn.

They glanced sideways at each other and broke into helpless snickers, and Shiro hummed a little laugh right along with them. This was… oh… dangerously comfortable, the way Marsh's mothers just *fit* so well together. The way they accepted Shiro as, perhaps not quite an equal since he didn't know enough, but as someone worth their time—it made him feel included, valued. So easy to think of the orchard as a cocoon of safety, a refuge from the life waiting out there for him.

The afternoon went quickly. Four harvesting bins filled with limes while Shiro tried to get his head bees under control. He went to the apartment while Dorae and Keira took the limes to Food Services, since they were adamant that nonunion people shouldn't deliver food.

With the resident AI assistant, a finch named Taktak, Shiro found children's learning modules on the local feeds and spent the rest of the time until dinner querying the basic information about station life that all resident children learned young. Guild history, he knew. The basic structure of Hansa society, so different from the stratified layers of the Imperium or the often-impenetrable bureaucratic swamp of ESTO. But the everyday life? He had no idea.

Marsh came for dinner again that evening and the atmosphere was as it had been before—warm and comforting, as Kiera and Dorae chose to tell stories about tiny Marsh trying to repair tools and take apart small electronics.

A bit of tension snuck into the air, though, when Marsh took Shiro's hand and said, "I think with the news story coming out, we should tell them."

Marsh's moms looked at each other and their son's hand on Shiro's before Keira pinned Marsh with worried eyes. "Tell us what, baby boy?"

"You remember we told you about how Shiro got here and the people who might be coming after him?" Marsh's hand tightened on Shiro's in a protective gesture.

"We remember. What is this?" Dorae's sharp gaze flicked between them. "You're scaring your Mama K."

"It's nothing horrible. It's just..." Marsh chewed on his lower lip, clearly not comfortable telling his mothers about the deception.

"This is my doing. Entirely." Shiro turned his palm so he could lace his fingers with Marsh's. "One of my more intimidating suitors ambushed us in the hallway. I panicked and told him Marsh and I were engaged. A news outlet's picked it up. Which, in a way is good, since I can't get a message out to my mother. Something's blocking channels, but the news service can get the story out, and she'll see it and know where I am." Shiro stopped his babbling and drew a slow breath. "So Marsh and I are pretend-engaged until Mother can send people for me."

Keira and Dorae both stared, Dorae verging on hostile.

"I'm... not sure how I feel about this." Keira shook her head sadly.

"Pretend, is it?" Dorae drummed her fingers on the counter, pointedly staring at their joined hands.

I think your son is wonderful. I wish I could marry him instead of all the people who've been paraded in front of me over the years. It's not going to help if I say that, is it? "We've agreed to be careful with each other. We *do* get along well."

"I needed you to know so you wouldn't see it on the nets first." Marsh's voice was soft, run through with tiny cracks. "Shiro needed help. It's not hurting anyone. Please say you won't give us away."

"He shouldn't be—" Dorae began, eyes bright with anger, but Keira put a hand on her arm to stop her.

"They're grown people. Remember what we're trying to work on."

"I remember," Dorae grumbled, clearly not mollified. "Let the boy live his life. But this…"

Kiera turned back to them with a sigh. "We're concerned. I think you both can understand that. We won't give you away, but be sure you don't take this too far. For both your sakes."

The backs of Shiro's eyes stung and he had to blink his vision clear. *For both our sakes. I think it's too late for me.* "I can't apologize enough for falling into your lives this way. And I can't thank you enough for being so kind. I think… I hope… that I've found a friend who won't vanish from my life once this is done."

There. That's the best I can do without falling apart or simply blurting out that I've developed feelings for your son.

"Of course you have." Marsh wrapped both hands around Shiro's. "We'll need to really start our own book club. Even if it's just the two of us. We need someone to listen when we want to complain about pretentious books."

Shiro tried to laugh, though it came out as more of a snort-hiccup. He breathed slowly, telling himself he had no right to fall apart now. Marsh's moms worried. Shiro had caused that and he couldn't bear to become more of an emotional burden. When he could trust his voice, he asked what he should have at the start of dinner. "How are your legs doing?"

"Not bad, really." Marsh glanced down at his legs as if they might help answer. "I spent a lot of time on my back trying to diagnose issues with the forever-glitching capacitors in the HVAC unit outside Ring Two's gathering hall."

Dorae snorted. "Again? They need to replace that thing."

"The administrators in Two are probably waiting until next cycle. They did have to do a refit on the AI assembly super-clean rooms." Keira waved her fork for emphasis before spearing a carrot slice.

"True." Marsh gave Shiro's hand a squeeze and slid off his stool. "I'll be back at it early tomorrow to finish, since their designated HVAC mechanic is out with broken fingers. So I'd better get me and my legs to bed."

He jogged around the corner to kiss first his Mama K's cheek, then his Mama D's, and with a determined glint in his eyes, jogged back around to kiss Shiro's as well. They said their good-nights, and Marsh left them staring uncomfortably at each other.

"You break his heart, it's not gonna matter how many soldier boys your mama surrounds you with," Dorae finally growled.

"Dorae, don't."

Shiro met her fierce gaze as best he could. "I don't want to. I'll try my best. I may not do as well with mine."

Dorae's forehead crinkled before she let out a gusty breath. "So that's how it is. Guess it's too late to save you from yourselves, then."

"Poor boys," Kiera whispered.

Their good-nights were subdued and solemn and under their sympathetic gazes. Shiro couldn't help but feel much younger than he was.

LATE THE NEXT MORNING, Marsh had finally finished work on the HVAC unit and found himself with the rest of the day to himself. He'd agreed to meet Shiro for lunch again in the starry concourse, and they could decide from there what to do with the rest of the day.

And wasn't that a strange thing? Another day where he was trying to think of something to entertain another person. When was the last time he'd *been* on a date? Not that this was dating. He had to stop slipping and thinking of it that way. Just keeping up appearances for those watching.

Marsh had no doubt people were. Made his skin crawl.

Up ahead, he spotted Shiro headed in the direction of Ring Three, easy to pick out of the lunchtime crowd, a bright flash amid more subdued work coveralls. The crowd thinned as they left the market areas of Ring Four until even the occasional person skating nearby had vanished and only Shiro remained, gliding leisurely up ahead.

Maybe skating behind him and watching the flash of butt and thighs under his tunic was a little creepy, so Marsh called out. "Shiro!"

His highness turned, gliding backward as he caught sight of Marsh and waved. Then a little Shiro grin tugged at his lips, spare and fleeting, before he made a beckoning gesture, turned back around and sped up.

"Oh, it's like that, is it?"

Marsh laughed and took off after him, keeping a close eye since Shiro flailed and wobbled a bit as he tried to skate faster. So much of his concentration centered on Shiro that he didn't see the man sitting on their bench in the concourse until he started to rise. By the way Shiro skidded to an uneven stop, barely keeping his balance, he hadn't spotted the bench poacher, either.

Tall, broad-shouldered, well-dressed, ship's boots —everything about him screamed *not local*, and all the hairs on Marsh's arms stood on end. *It can't be…*

"Shiro." The man spoke softly, with a confidence that said he rarely had to raise his voice. "There you are."

Marsh caught up in time to hear Shiro whisper, "He can't be here." Instead of answering the man, he turned to Marsh and gripped his arm. "How is he *here*? Without an alert? How did he get onstation?"

"I don't—" Marsh squinted down the concourse, then checked his messages in case he'd missed something. "Is that Hengist?"

Shiro's eyes were trying to take over his entire face,

muscles trembling in his tight jaw. Possible that he couldn't get his teeth apart to answer, but he managed a nod. Gally scurried down to the floor and did an arched-back-ferret threat dance at Hengist.

"I don't know how you got past Immigration since you're red-flagged." Marsh lifted his chin in his best attempt at defiance. "And you're not allowed within a hundred meters of Shiro."

The smile Hengist gave him was as soft as his voice. Marsh couldn't even call it an evil smile. Maybe a little condescending, but shouldn't it have been more menacing? Malicious?

"It's not difficult to present a false identity." Hengist shrugged, as if a treaty offense was something negligible. "Come in under another name. Leave the gunships standing out far enough not to ping. No flags go up."

A shuffle behind Marsh pulled his head around. Three large men blocked the walkway behind them. *Goons. Like in a drama vid.*

Shiro pulled Marsh closer. The black cylinder was in his hand again. "What do you want?"

"My love, you need to grow up a bit. No wonder your mother was so desperate to find you a husband. All this nonsense running about the galaxy. Broadcasting a fictional love story."

"It's not fictional," Shiro snarled, the conviction in his voice giving Marsh chills.

"Suit yourself." Hengist turned his smile on Marsh. "We know it's fictional, don't we? Because there are rules and procedures for being affianced to a prince. Centuries-old customs. Which I have navigated and you have not." The smile stayed fixed, but the voice grew colder than the black outside the concourse windows. "Your mother promised you to *me*, Shiro. And you will honor that promise. Now."

"Your delusions have only grown more pronounced." Shiro powered down the mag-lev on his boots, his stance now stable and surprisingly aggressive. "Mother promised you nothing. I certainly didn't choose you. And I'm not going anywhere."

"Always so difficult. I appreciate that you've made me work for it, but enough people have been hurt because of your insistence on this game of chase. Enough, love. It's quite enough." Hengist waved a hand at his men. "Gentlemen, secure his highness. Separate him from the stationer."

Shiro shoved Marsh away, putting himself in the path of the advancing goons. "Stay behind me, Marsh. Please."

Marsh ignored him, mostly, too busy tapping out the emergency signal on his link. *Assault. Illegal contact. Battery in progress.* It would take Judiciary personnel a few minutes to get to them, but as long as he finished the message, they would have his location. "Help's coming, Shiro. Don't… do anything."

But the moment the two front goons seized Shiro's arms, the panic in his eyes told Marsh he might as well have stayed quiet. The third goon came around and took hold of Marsh. He wasn't planning on putting up a fight, though his boots squeaked as they skidded.

Then Shiro let out a rage-laden scream and too many things happened for Marsh to keep track of. Marsh's goon lifted him off his feet and hurled him into the walkway's railing. He hit with a sickening crunch and landed in a heap on the floor, his limbnet sparking and his legs seizing from the agony of neural signals gone haywire. His link lay in shards on the concourse plating.

His view wasn't a good one, and pain might've been making him delirious, but he thought Shiro was somehow wielding lightning, his fluid, practiced movements making the goons clumsy in comparison. Shiro hooked an ankle around one man's leg and sent him crashing to the floor. Then he flicked his wrist, and a short sword switchbladed from the metal cylinder in his right hand, which he whipped about too fast for Marsh to follow, sparks leaping wherever he hit.

In no more than three or four slices of his arm, Shiro had all three men flat on the ground. He raced to Marsh, heaved him over one shoulder, and ran at Hengist with a feral roar. One more lightning strike with the flat of Shiro's blade, and Hengist was down as well, flopping on the walkway like someone too drunk to stand.

Shiro waited long enough for Gally to climb to his head, then took off running toward Ring Three, Marsh's head bouncing against his back.

"Where do we hide?" Shiro called over his shoulder. "Marsh? Someplace unexpected. They won't be down long."

"Door… slow down… hold on… Shiro!" Marsh called out desperately.

Shiro halted long enough to shift Marsh into his arms. "Where?"

"There." Marsh panted through the pain in his legs. "Service access. Here… palm."

It took a moment's maneuvering, but Shiro

managed to hold Marsh up to place his palm in the lock. The door slid open and Shiro hurried them inside. When the access panel closed, Shiro placed Marsh on the floor, his face gray and stricken.

"No, oh no. Marsh…" Shiro's hands hovered, all the ferocity from a second before drained away. "What do I do? Your legs, oh goddess. How do we stop it?"

"Don't panic." Marsh held up his shaking hands. "I need you… turn the net off. Can't… myself. Right knee. Side. Little depress. That's… yeah… there."

The sparking died as Shiro shut the stupid thing down. Marsh pulled in a sobbing breath, the relief almost as painful as the damaged net. Shiro's sob melded with his as he pulled Marsh into his arms, rocking him in little fits and starts.

"I'm so sorry. I'm so so sorry. You weren't supposed to be… I should never have… Oh, I'm so sorry…"

"Hey." Marsh managed to wrap shaking arms around him, stroking his hair. "I'm okay. A little bruised, probably. But I'm okay. Now that the limbnet's off, it's much better. What about you? What the crud *was* that back there?"

"They were—"

"I know what they were doing. You had lightning in your hand. A lightning *sword*."

"Oh. That." Shiro had to take a few breaths, getting himself back under control. "Probably the least elegant raiwakizashi demonstration in history."

"Is it an old military weapon or something?" Marsh snuggled into Shiro's arms. "I saw articles with you and raiwakizashi competitions."

"It's traditional, yes. From the Corporation War

days. An electrified sword used in fencing. Though today, I was using it more like a glorified shock stick."

"Hey, it worked. They were serious about their violence. And you got us out of there."

Shiro heaved a shuddering sigh and kissed the top of Marsh's head. "I should never have put you in that position. Never."

"You didn't know that would happen. *I'm* the one who told you that you were safe."

"Hmm. Not your fault." Shiro's voice was small and hopeful as he asked, "Do you think your message got through?"

Marsh stroked Shiro's arm, feeling the little tremors there. "Not sure. But we're all right here for a bit. Let me rest a minute. I'll see if I can do a patch on the limbnet. And we'll see what we want to do then."

After a few moments silence, Shiro spoke softly, his breath warm against Marsh's hair. "I'm glad you're with me this time. I wish you weren't, but I'm still glad you're here."

"I'm a little scared, since that made perfect sense."

CHAPTER EIGHT

Shiro's head swam with thoughts of his siblings—how in the same situation, any one of them would have a Plan with many Steps and Contingencies. They'd also have better weapons and wouldn't have abandoned their guard attachments, either, so that wasn't a terribly constructive thing for his brain to obsess over.

When his shuddering had subsided, Marsh had fallen asleep with his head in Shiro's lap. Presumably, painful neurological disruptions took a lot out of a person. They were safe here for a bit, so Shiro didn't mind being a pillow. His legs had fallen asleep and he had to remind himself sternly every few minutes not to stroke Marsh's short curls—he hadn't received permission—but those were small discomforts. Without any access to comm, though, how would they know when it *was* safe to emerge?

It wasn't possible to judge the passage of time by the clicks and tocks of the pipes surrounding them. Gally probably could, but the ferret had curled up and plugged into what appeared to be a recharging station. Still, Shiro thought it couldn't have been more than an hour before Marsh opened his eyes again.

"Hi." Marsh's smile made Shiro catch his breath. It was so beautiful, so sweet, and just for him.

He managed to get the fluttering in his stomach under control enough to say, "Hello. How are you feeling?"

"Not bad, considering." Marsh struggled into a sitting position, scooting around so he could lean against the pipes and pulled the strap of his bag off over his head. "Okay. First order of business. Legs."

He fished in the bag, brought out what must have been the food containers for lunch, and undid a roll of delicate tools on the floor beside him. Whistling softly through his teeth, he picked up a tiny bit of metal that resembled a bent crowbar, pulled the right leg of his coveralls up over his knee, and opened a panel on his leg half the size of his palm.

Shiro sucked in a breath. "Does that hurt?"

"What? Oh. No." Marsh shook his head with a little chuckle. "It's just an add-on for the operating system. It just *looks* like part of me. They did a really good job on the dermal matching." He reached for a pen light, moving his leg with his free hand for a better angle. "I haven't had to do this for a while, though. It's stupidly awkward."

"Can I help you?"

Marsh glanced over, blinking at Shiro in a distracted way. "Maybe? I feel like I need five hands. Could you hold the light? No, more to the left. Steady. Yes. Right there."

Fascinating to watch, the sure movements of

Marsh's hands as he took up a tiny pair of pliers and extracted components from within that Shiro vaguely recognized as belonging to a circuit matrix. The net itself lay in barely visible silver lines along Marsh's brown skin, the material of the lines—metal, composite, or possibly bio-fusion—molded seamlessly to his skin.

"You were magnificent, you know," Marsh offered after he found a replacement component in his bag and had managed to click it in place. "Fighting off those goons. I've never seen anyone move that fast."

Shiro's face heated, and he struggled to keep the light steady. "We're taught self-defense almost as soon as we can walk. Basics of tactical command come a little later, but not much."

"Don't you always have soldiers with you? Bodyguards?" Marsh frowned as he started packing his tools away. "Why would you need that?"

"Because there's always the possibility that we could be separated from them." Shiro put a hand over his heart. "Case in point. Above all else, the imperial line must be preserved. That's what we're taught."

The implication of *had it bashed into our heads as toddlers* was clear, but Marsh was kind enough not to mention it. Although, as he closed up his leg panel, he did say, "I hope you won't be offended, but it kinda sounds like a restrictive childhood."

"Hmm. It had its moments." Shiro clicked off the light and handed it to Marsh. "But beyond the normal decorum expectations for any child in the spotlight, the need to protect ourselves, the expectation to excel at something, and the obligation to reproduce? I count myself lucky that my family has always been supportive of who I am. Not every child in the galaxy has that luxury."

"Right." Marsh stared at his leg a moment. "I hadn't thought about it like that. But if you could do that—the thing you did on the concourse—why wait until now if he's been harassing you?"

"He wasn't physically violent, not before Ceti Tau. Attacking him without cause would be a potential diplomatic nightmare. When he *did* attack the compound, I never caught sight of him. Hand-to-hand skills aren't terribly effective against distance weapons." Shiro gave Marsh a moment—he seemed deep in thought—before he asked, "Do you think it's fixed? Your limbnet?"

"Maybe. Only one way to find out."

Asking *are you sure* would've been insulting to Marsh's skills, so Shiro settled for holding his breath and staying ready to pounce and turn the limbnet off again if Marsh showed any signs of distress. A faint hum joined the whirs and clicks of the service access corridor before it faded.

Shiro counted to ten before he spoke. "Everything feels normal?"

"No sparky agony issues, which is a good start." Marsh let out a laugh that startled them both. "I'll have to report the damage. Ugh. Forms. Should bump me up the list, though."

"I would hope so. It's probably not the right thing to offer to buy one for you, is it?"

Marsh shook his head, not angry but definitely no longer laughing. "No. They're complex neural assist devices that have to be made specifically for each person, and there are only so many they can make at once. If someone needs one more than I do, they need to have theirs manufactured first."

Shiro took both of Marsh's hands, gently, running his thumbs over the backs. "It's not how things work here. I know that. But I really want to say you're more important and should have yours and to hell with everyone else. Is that horrible?"

"Not horrible. Just worried, I'd guess." Marsh leaned in to kiss his cheek. "Thank you for worrying."

"You're welcome," Shiro whispered out of habit, his skin on fire where Marsh's lips had touched down. He kept hold of Marsh's hands, pulling him closer. "I know this is beyond ridiculous and the absolute worst possible timing. But I… I hope I haven't scared you off. That is… you know I want you… don't you?"

"It's so hard not to tease you right now." Marsh ran a finger over Shiro's jaw. "And say something like, *Really? I had no idea.* But that kiss yesterday said it in five-meter-high letters."

Shiro shifted uncomfortably, staring at the floor. "Marsh…"

"Of course I want you, too. Did you doubt it?" Marsh's smile turned shy. "And you didn't scare me. You going all martial arts on those goons was, um, it was kinda hot."

"Was it?" Shiro leaned their foreheads together, unable to stop his fall into Marsh's gravity well. "Should I assault threatening minions more often?"

"Don't you dare." Marsh scooted around so he could wrap his arms around Shiro and rest his head on his shoulder. "The imperium might want you safe, but so do I."

"Oh."

The words lanced through Shiro, little pinpricks of heat that gathered into a ball at his core. Marsh found him not only desirable but also impressive, which no man ever had, and worried for him, which few people who weren't family or weren't paid to had ever done.

He ran his hands up and down Marsh's back in long, soothing strokes, all too keenly aware of the layers of cloth between them. Fewer clothes would be wonderful, even if his skin already jumped and twitched. Even if nothing happened—and the location was *not* one he would have picked for a first time with Marsh—he could drink in the contact, the closeness of these moments.

Marsh's fingers found the hem of his tunic, and Shiro's breath caught as they skimmed up, tracing heat along his ribs.

"This okay?"

For a few heartbeats, Shiro adjusted to that touch, the shivering along his skin settling when Marsh didn't grow immediately more aggressive or try to reach higher. He pulled in a long breath and whispered, "Yes."

Their lips met on that breath, tentative exploration quickly catching fire. Marsh's sounds spoke of desperation—maybe it had been a while—and Shiro took the lead when he hesitated, running his tongue over the seam of Marsh's lips, gentle but insistent. Marsh opened on a moan that vibrated through Shiro's bones. *This* was what he'd felt in that kiss the day before. This immediate, fire-laced connection that seared him from the inside out and yet settled him like no one's touch ever had.

He slid a hand down Marsh's throat, toying with the fastener pull on his coveralls. "Yes?"

"Yes," Marsh whispered in answer, his lips tracing the line of Shiro's jaw while his hand encouraged Shiro's on the fastening, which parted on a whisper of biopoly.

Shiro parted the fabric, running his fingers through the tight curls of Marsh's chest hair.

"Is it all right?" Marsh blurted out. "Not everyone likes—"

With a little hum, Shiro kissed his collarbone. "I like the chest hair because it's yours. It's perfect."

Marsh moaned out something unintelligible when Shiro skimmed his fingertips over one brown nipple. He caught Shiro's hands, breaths coming in little sips. "Shiro… we should talk about things. What you like. And don't like. And… well…"

"Is this the top or bottom question?" Shiro stopped nuzzling at Marsh's chest fur to meet his eyes. He couldn't help a little smile at the anxiety there. "Perhaps we keep that for next time? I do like a variety of things, but I don't have any of my cocks with me. Or any other necessities, for that matter."

"Next time?" Marsh asked, the words trembling between them.

"Yes. There will be one." Shiro hooked his fingers under his tunic hem and lifted it over his head, surprising himself by continuing with, "Say it for me. There's going to be a next time."

Marsh chuckled as he ran lazy fingers along Shiro's ribs. "You're bossy during sex. Okay. There's going to be a next time. I really want there to be."

He didn't sound entirely like he believed it, but it

was a good start. Shiro had no intention of walking away when he was safe and never seeing Marsh again. The thought hit him hard and fierce when he'd said it. It wasn't possible. They weren't possible. Everyone would say so.

For once, Shiro wasn't going to simply sit back and let others tell him what was possible. Marsh wanted a next time.

"You're beautiful. I know you hear that a lot." Marsh struggled out of the sleeves of his coveralls and wriggled the material down to his thighs. "Doesn't make it less true."

Shiro stared down at his hands and came to a decision. He yanked off his boots, tugged the tie free on his loose pants, and slid out of them. It took trust to do it in a brightly lit space with someone he hadn't been with before, but he trusted Marsh more than he did his own brothers.

"I didn't believe it when people told me so. Not when I was young. All my siblings grew up so gracefully while I was awkward. Not comfortable in my body yet." He rose up on his knees and set his pants aside, letting Marsh look as he pleased. "And now when they say it, I wonder what they want from me. But I… it feels real when you say it."

Marsh lay back and held his hands out. "Come here. Please."

"No, not yet." Shiro gave a mock-serious nod to the dark-red briefs still covering Marsh.

"Sorry. Gods." Marsh wriggled those down to his knees as well. "Better?"

Shiro let out a deep, appreciative sigh. Taken altogether, Marsh was… perfect. He was stuck on the word because it was true. Compact, lean-muscled, with a lovely black treasure trail that started just above his navel and his cock straight and proudly erect on his stomach—perfect.

With a soft hum of laughter at the situation, Shiro folded his tunic and slid it behind Marsh's head. "I hope that's better. This can't be too comfortable."

"It's not bad." Marsh held his hands out again for Shiro to take. "The floor's smooth here, and I'm not lying on any rivets."

"Small favors." Shiro accepted his steadying hands as he straddled Marsh's thighs. "Do you know you're a work of art?"

Marsh's smile crooked to one side, possibly in embarrassment. "The apocalyptic plant-life kind?"

"Goddess, no. I'd paint you in oils." Shiro kissed his palm. "Sketch you in pencils."

"You'd have to get me to sit still long enough." Marsh tugged him forward. "No more hovering. You're killing me."

"Oh, and *I'm* the bossy one."

Shiro laughed, shocking himself with the volume of it, and lowered himself atop Marsh. He gasped at the heat coming off of Marsh, the pleasure almost too sharp as so much skin met his at once. Shiro's thighs trembled, keeping their groins apart as he adjusted to the onslaught of sensation, while Marsh stroked his back, making it clear that he wouldn't rush Shiro.

"Okay there?" Marsh whispered against his ear, sending a delicious shiver down his back.

"Yes. It's…sometimes, it's too much. High-voltage nerve endings, and I have to wait until some of the amperage dissipates."

Marsh's chuckle vibrated through him. "That's very sweet."

"Is it?"

"Yes. You tailoring your metaphors just for me."

Shiro pulled back with a frown. "It wasn't intention—oh, you're teasing."

"Just trying to distract you a little. You got all tense."

In answer, Shiro bent his head for a kiss, his tongue stroking Marsh's serving as another distraction as he lowered himself. The contact had them both gasping, so Marsh wasn't as calm as he appeared. Their cocks rubbing together was exquisite, and the overactive stabs of pleasure settled quickly into a purring hum. Shiro spread his thighs for more weight, more contact, and Marsh tipped his head back with a soft moan.

Shiro thrust his hips, rubbing them together, increasingly powerful zips of pleasure spearing him as he hit just the right angle. Marsh's hands slid down Shiro's ribs to grip his ass, dragging a long answering moan from him.

"Shiro…"

It sounded like a question, so Shiro sucked at the base of Marsh's jaw to encourage him, whispering, "It's glorious, just, oh…"

Marsh thrust his hips in time with Shiro's. The pleasure built in a steady rhythm that soon became a rushing wave, an avalanche. Shiro clung tight and rode Marsh harder, gasping moans shorter and louder.

"Gods… Shiro…" Marsh groaned into his hair. "I can't… I'm coming."

A hundred things might have occurred to Shiro

with other lovers. Where the mess would be. Whether clothes were in the way. For Marsh, there was only, "*Yes.*"

The heat of Marsh coming against his stomach shoved Shiro over, his orgasm hitting him in waves so hard and sharp that he shook, the world whiting out around him for a half breath. He rested his head on Marsh's shoulder, sprawled atop him, listening to their breaths quiet and synch. Here in Marsh's arms, he fit, as he had nowhere else in the galaxy.

I can't leave this. Can't leave him. *I can't go home and never have this again. There's a way. There will be a way.*

"Are your legs all right?" he asked when he'd caught his breath.

"Legs?" Marsh murmured sleepily. "What legs?"

"Do you need me to roll off?"

"Stay. You're so warm. Legs are fine."

Shiro chose to believe him and snuggled into a more comfortable position. He'd begun to drift off when a strange three-note whistle sounded in the access space. His head jerked up, heart pounding.

"What was that?"

Marsh stroked his back. "Station all-comm. Shh. There'll be a message."

The whistle sounded a second time, followed by a clear, melodic voice over the station's systems, "Prince Shiro. Prince Shiro Shinohara. Please report to Immigration immediately. Prince Shiro, please report to Immigration. Thank you."

CHAPTER NINE

"Could it be a trick?" Shiro had sat up, clutching his pants in both hands.

Marsh shook his head. "No. I mean that was Madelena in the comm section. Everyone knows her voice. But I don't know why they'd call you down there."

Shiro still stared at the speaker. He shook himself and glanced down at the mess of spunk on his chest and stomach. "It's, hmm, the most likely explanation is someone's come from my mother. It's a shame there's no shower in here."

"I can't get you that, but I wouldn't be much of a mechanic if I didn't keep clean rags in my bag." Marsh dragged the bag toward him by the strap, fished around, and handed Shiro one soft cloth while he took another for himself. It hurt that the anxiety was back in Shiro's eyes. Marsh moved deliberately and calmly so he wouldn't make it worse.

"He's going to still be out there. Waiting." Shiro's hands trembled as he hurried to wipe himself down and get dressed. "But I can't stay here. Not if there's a possibility Altairian marines are looking for me."

"Right. We need to get you to Immigration, and we need a plan." Marsh, whose boots were still on, was dressed first with a quick refastening of his coveralls. "We'll go back to my quarters—"

Shiro shook his head in short, jerking movements. "No. No, we can't. He'll have found out where you live by now. I'm sure he has some way. He'll assume we'll go there."

"He might have men stationed a bunch of places." Marsh chewed on his lower lip. "But we can't just sit here while things get ugly with marines when you don't show up."

Still thinking hard, Marsh helped Shiro with his second boot and enveloped him in a hard hug. Breathing Shiro's scent calmed him, giving him a few moments when his brain wasn't running in circles. A sudden memory hit, jolting his entire body.

"What is it?" Shiro leaned back, searching his face. "Marsh… you have an idea, don't you?"

"I do. It might even work." Marsh offered a grin as he helped Shiro up. "We need to get to the closest central node and make a quick call. Then we need to run like hell for the tube access and head for Immigration."

Shiro flicked his wrist, and his lightning sword reappeared in his right hand. "All right. I'll do my best to protect you. The last thing I want is for you to be hurt again."

"Last resort. Please, sweetheart." Marsh kissed him softly and leaned their foreheads together. "I don't want you hurt, either."

"All right." Shiro hesitated before he said, "You, ah, called me sweetheart."

"I did. You're adorable when the tops of your ears blush, and we'll have to talk about it later, okay?"

Shiro gave him a sharp nod and strode to the door. "Let me go first in case they've figured out where we went."

"Kind of unlikely? But let Gally take a quick peek first." Gally bounced up from the recharging port and galumphed to them. "Gally, stay low. Just take a quick peek both ways."

They took opposite sides of the doorway, Shiro crouched low on his side of the frame. Marsh hit the palm lock and stood frozen while Gally flattened themself to the floor and peered out into the corridor. After looking both ways, Gally bounced up and to *chek* at them.

"It's clear. Which way?"

Marsh scooped his ferret up and draped them over his shoulders. "To your right. We have to backtrack a little to the central node."

Hand in hand, they shot out of the access way and skated off as fast as Shiro could manage. Still a lot faster than any human could run. The few people they passed were neighbors of Marsh's who offered waves as they went about their own workdays. No ominous figures lurking in cross corridors. No running footsteps behind them. Not yet.

"Marsh!" A familiar voice called from behind them. "Hold up!"

He half-turned to see Ruba skating madly to catch up to them. Marsh slowed them but didn't stop, waiting until Ruba skated beside them before he said, "What's up?"

"Your boyfriend's got stalkers, right? I saw the asylum bulletin."

"Yes. Okay, yes. Why?"

She turned to him briefly, eyes huge. "These scary nonstationers came into my depot about an hour ago. They wanted mag-lev boots. I told them I didn't have any, even though they tried to get up in my face and shout me down. I thought they might be… Well, I lied to them so they wouldn't have any. Was I right?"

He gripped her arm in a thank-you and got them all skating faster. "You were so right. Go, Ruba. You don't want to be with us right now. I'm calling in a Lia Kish."

She shot him a fierce grin and bent her knees for a sharp turn at the next cross corridor. "Be careful, you two!"

"We have a speed advantage, then," Shiro murmured. "We might make it."

The closest central node loomed in front of them after the next right turn. Smooth pillars painted bright blue to make them easier to spot, they provided secure comm to emergency services on separate power sources and trunks in case of localized outages and housed fire-suppression and first-aid supplies. Also, if a stationer knew how, the node could serve as personal comm if said stationer's comm had been, say, smashed by thugs. While Marsh had considered calling emergency services, that would mean they'd be waiting at the node for Judiciary workers to arrive, which kept them in one place far too long and got them no closer to Immigration.

When they reached the pillar, Shiro skidded to a stop beside him, alert and determined, watching the corridors in all directions. *My valiant prince.* Marsh smiled at the thought as he brought up the interface and went through log-in procedures, then the directory, since the call codes programmed into his personal comm weren't ones he'd memorized.

"Who's this?" Mama D growled through the speaker.

"It's Marsh. Please just listen." Marsh pulled in a deep breath. "We're in trouble. Outsiders are after us. I don't think we have long. Do you remember Lia Kish? And what everyone did when Adanai bounty hunters came for her? We need that now."

For a moment silence answered him, and Marsh worried that he might have to explain in detail. But Mama K's voice came through next. "Go, baby boy. We got you. Get to Immigration. We'll meet you there."

Marsh cut the connection and took Shiro's hand again, the warmth and the quick squeeze of fingers steadying him. "Okay. Back the way we came. The tube access is only a level down, three cross corridors, and a couple hundred meters from here."

"What are your mothers going to do?" Shiro balked, forehead crinkled in concern.

"Come on." Marsh tugged to get them moving. "If it works, it's easier to explain once you see."

They took off again, only slowing for the ramp to the next level down. Taking the ramps at high speed on mag-lev boots was what kids did—and caused some spectacular accidents. Just one cross corridor to go, and some of the tension left Marsh's shoulders.

They'd made it without being spotted. *Now just to get to the tube access panel and program a cube for—*

A shout went up behind them, joined by another. Marsh sped up again, his heart slamming against his chest, Shiro keeping up gamely but throwing wild-eyed looks over his shoulder. The echoes off the empty corridor made it sound like a pack of hunting dogs from a historical vid drama were chasing them. Marsh risked a quick look. Three large men raced out of the last cross corridor and took after them. They'd been watching the tube access closest to the concourse where Shiro had left them sprawled on the deck plates.

Of course they had.

Marsh let go of Shiro and threw himself toward the panel at top speed. He hit the wall beside it with a hard thud and was already punching in a program to get them to Immigration when he yelled back, "Keep them off us, Shiro! We just need to get in a cube!"

Jaw set, Shiro turned, still gliding toward Marsh as he stopped and turned off his boots. The raiwakizashi in his hand hummed and sparked as he swept it in a threatening arc toward their pursuers. Marsh caught their hesitation out of the corner of his eye as they slowed and approached more warily. One man crept too close and Shiro lunged, sweeping the weapon toward him, the lightning arcing down his arm. That thug stumbled back, crying out in pain.

Marsh watched the indicators, willing the cubes to hurry. They didn't, of course. They always moved at the same speed. *Just a couple seconds more, just a couple...*

The thugs tried a coordinated attack. Again, Shiro sliced the air, leaving lightning in his wake, forcing them to retreat. One of the thugs pulled a gun. The tube access pinged. Shiro backed up against Marsh. The doors opened and Marsh grabbed a double handful of Shiro's tunic. The thug fired. Marsh flung himself headfirst into the cube, yanking Shiro in behind him. They landed on the floor in a tangled disoriented heap when the cube took off and slammed them against the back wall.

A burnt smell had entered the cube with them.

"Shiro!" Marsh righted himself, turning Shiro, desperate to see if he had been hit. His *sleeve* was smoking. "Did he get you? Are you okay?"

"I'm… oh, dear." Shiro's face went unquestionably gray. He turned his arm for a better look. "Ah. Well. Could have been worse, I suppose."

A tight-beam shot had raked Shiro's right arm, the burned line of skin red and blistering. Marsh got as much of his sleeve out of the way as possible and decided the best thing would be to leave it alone for someone qualified to deal with.

"Is it bad?"

"I think once the adrenaline wears off it could well be painful." Shiro swallowed hard. "I'm fine for now."

They huddled together on the floor of the cube as it zipped around the station, neither one willing to move.

"How did you think they got weapons onstation?"

Marsh tipped his head at Shiro. "How did you get yours in?"

"Mine was in my bag." Shiro shifted to watch their progress on the readout over the door. "You brought it to me. It's not as if it went through Customs." He chewed on his lower lip a moment. "Oh. I see. They smuggled something in through a repair bay or something similar."

"Probably. Or they had a miniature fabricator shipped in, supposedly for something else, and just printed one."

"That would be clever. I suppose Hengist is rather, though not the sort of clever I really admire." Shiro rested his head on Marsh's shoulder. He'd started to shiver and Marsh wished they had a blanket. "Tell me about Lia Kish," Shiro said through his shuddering.

Marsh put an arm around him to keep him steady. "Right. Lia immigrated here because her husband didn't want her working in ceramics engineering. There are some places in the Adanai Collective, isolated ones, where the marriage laws are really one-sided and strange. She filed her divorce with the Central Adanai Courts and left him. He… to say he was upset would be a huge understatement. He sent bounty hunters to bring her back. They got onstation, probably under false names. Never really thought about it much before."

"That's terrible. What did she do?"

"It's what the station did. I'm hoping you'll see in a minute." Marsh checked the readouts. "There's a cube right behind us. It's been following our same tube path the whole way."

"That has to be them. How did they…? Oh. No. That's a silly question." Shiro sighed. "*Everyone* onstation knows where I'm going."

"They do," Marsh agreed softly as he helped Shiro stand. *Please, please let this have worked.*

Shiro's attention flicked between the readouts

above and the cube's door. "They'll be seconds behind us, won't they? We'll have to run again."

"Maybe. Do you think you can if we have to?"

"I'm not sure. Marsh…" Shiro leaned into him harder. "If I can't, you need to run. You have nothing to do with this. I… you can't put yourself in danger for me any more than you have."

"The hell you say." Marsh snorted. "I'm staying with you to make sure no one tosses you into a crate and carts you away. Shiro, look at me. It's going to be okay."

Shiro turned his head toward Marsh, lashes clinging together with moisture as he blinked rapidly. "Don't do this. Please. I lo—"

The cube emitted a series of chimes, the approach warning for their destination. Marsh put a hand under the elbow of Shiro's good arm and wrapped his free arm tight around Shiro's waist, leaning against the wall for support as the cube decelerated.

"Get ready."

His fear that the doors would open on an empty corridor only intensified as they waited out the seconds for the cube to come to a full stop. The chime sounded for the doors opening. Marsh found he was holding his breath as he stepped carefully out of the cube, watching his feet, with Shiro tucked tight against his side.

The silence chilled him to his bones. *It didn't work.*

Beside him, Shiro let out a gasp. "Marsh…"

When Marsh lifted his head, he blinked at the sight in front of him. Stationers lined the corridor on either side, dozens and dozens of them.

"Oh thank gods," he breathed out. "Thank you. Thank you all so much for coming."

Donya from Medical Aid smiled on Marsh's right and hustled him away from the cube. "Thank us later. Get going, you two. We've got this."

As they moved forward, people closed in behind them, blocking the corridor entirely. Another rank and another rank for every step they took until it was difficult to see the tube access point.

"Marsh? What's happening here?" Shiro scanned the crowd with wide eyes.

"This is the Lia Kish defense. The community doesn't take kindly to outsiders threatening their own, and the community responds."

"This is amazing," Shiro whispered as he nodded thanks to the people they passed. "Just amazing."

The tube access chimed behind them and Marsh tried to get them moving faster. It would be all right, though. Now everything really would be all right. Up to a point.

"Out of the way!" a rough voice bellowed. "That man's a wanted criminal!"

A sound of a scuffle broke out by the access, but the stationers didn't react, calmly closing ranks, row upon row, as Marsh and Shiro passed.

"He has a weapon!" someone shouted. It sounded like Donya.

The noises of fighting increased, and Marsh risked a look back to see the three thugs go down under a sea of civilians. He was relieved when the scuffle subsided without a shot fired. While all the bodies blocked the view, he had no doubt that those thugs were being sat on until Judiciary could get there. They turned the first corner, their path marked out by the stationers lining the way. Even if they had been separated for some reason, Shiro wouldn't have had any chance of getting lost.

"How did this happen?" Shiro asked as Marsh waved to the salvage bay crew. "How did your mothers do this so fast?"

"Contact networks. Work group messaging. Snagging people in the hallway." Marsh grinned and accepted elbow bumps from a row of mechanic's apprentices. "You hit up a few people really fast, and the whole station knows in minutes."

"It's just… I've never seen anything like this. People just spontaneously working together. And it's…" Shiro's voice cracked. "It's for us."

"It is." Marsh gave him a gentle squeeze, bursting with pride for his station.

At the next cross corridor, another shout went up, "Let me *through*! That young man is my fiancé and he's seriously ill! You have to stop him!"

"Hengist," Shiro muttered through clenched teeth.

Of course, no one stopped them. Then a bellow drowned out Hengist's lies and demands. "Hengist McClain, you will turn and face me!"

"Who was *that*?" Marsh turned his head, though he had no chance of seeing what was happening.

Shiro's eyes were huge as he answered in a shocked voice. "That… that was Goro Rin."

Help from all sides. Who would've thought?

Hands urged them on, the ranks closing behind them even faster.

"Go on, Marsh! Go, go!" became a chant as they hurried toward the entrance to Immigration. The three-meter-high arched doors slid open as they approached, and a different kind of cacophony hit them when the doors slid shut behind them.

"Marsh! Thank gods, we saw the vid…"

"Are you all right, baby boy?"

"Highness!"

"Goddess, he's hurt."

"Call Medical."

"How bad is it?"

"Have him sit down."

A broad-shouldered woman in body armor expertly peeled Marsh away from Shiro and guided him to the nearest bench in the Immigration vestibule. Before he could even register the loss, arms engulfed Marsh, Mama D cursing softly and Mama K crying on his shoulder.

"Hey, I'm okay. No crying." Marsh turned to try to hug them both at once, close to tears of relief himself.

"Judiciary had a vid," Mama K hiccupped through her words. "Those horrible men…they…*threw* you."

"We knew from your call location which tube access you'd take." Mama K still frowned at everyone else around them, warning them back. "So at least we knew where to start the line. But we didn't know until we got down here what'd happened."

"I'm just a little bruised." Marsh tried to disentangle, but they were holding on too tight. His laugh may have held an edge of hysteria. "Moms!"

Mama D relented. "We saw your leg sparking."

"Yeah, bit of a short. I fixed it."

"Uh-huh." A world of skepticism and recrimination existed in those two syllables.

He kissed Mama K's cheek and managed to step

back. "I need to see how Shiro's doing. I'm not going anywhere. One of those jackasses shot him."

"*What?*" Mama D roared, and of course they had to tromp across the space with him to where Shiro now sat surrounded by large, looming people in body armor.

One of them turned, a young woman with dark eyes and a rasping voice, and held a warning hand up. "Keep back, please."

"Yuki." Shiro's voice came from within the bodyguard cocoon. "Let Marsh through, please."

The armored shell parted just far enough for Marsh to squeeze through before closing again. He plunked next to Shiro and took the hand on his uninjured side. "Holding up?"

The soft hum of Shiro's laugh was more of a comfort than Marsh wanted to admit. "I'd like to be brave and say everything's fine, but I'm afraid I'm not. Rather painful, actually."

"Medics are coming, highness," the larger blonde woman offered. "ETA in three minutes."

"Thank you." Shiro heaved a sigh and leaned against Marsh. "Have I said yet what a relief it is to see you, Sergeant Hana? You're here. You're whole. Did we have any casualties?"

"Highness." Sergeant Hana gave him an abbreviated bow. "Your concern, as always, does you credit. Minor injuries. Your full complement is onstation."

"Thank goddesses. I felt terrible deserting you."

The stern face cracked a wicked smile. "You didn't really think a bunch of mercs could take us, did you? No harm, highness. It was our duty to guard your retreat, and it was your duty to escape to safety."

"Hmm, yes. Honor and duty. Sergeant Hana, this is Marsh Kensinger." Shiro pointed with their joined hands. "Marsh, Sergeant Pepper Hana and Corporals Jacob Kiro and Yuki Saito."

"Oh, the fiancé," Corporal Kiro blurted out.

Corporal Saito kicked him, whispering, "That's fake, you idiot."

Of course he knew it, but that kick felt like it had hit Marsh's stomach. Still, he managed as much of a smile as he could. "Nice to meet you all. Shiro really has been worried about you."

He received three smart military bows for that. Altairian marines really were scary sexy like everyone said.

Pleasantries over, Sergeant Hana was all business once more. "Highness, would you be able to identify the man who shot you?"

"Yes." Shiro nodded slowly. "That is, I think he was aiming for Marsh. But yes, I saw him clearly."

"I don't care if he was aiming for the nearest *asteroid*. He shot a prince of the blood. That can't go unanswered." Sergeant Hana huffed a breath. "Your highness."

"Duly noted." Shiro lifted his head from Marsh's shoulder. "Ah. I think the medics are trying to get through your blockade."

Marsh moved over far enough to let the medics work but didn't leave the bench. They removed bits of sleeve from the burn with care, covered it with something greasy looking, covered that with plaskin, and pronounced Shiro would be fine if he left it alone and kept it dry.

Whatever they'd slathered on the burn must have had a strong analgesic in it, too, since the tightness eased around Shiro's eyes, and the gray faded from his complexion. He stood, steady on his feet again, and turned his bodyguards to introduce them to Marsh's moms. Polite, yes, but Marsh had a feeling it was also how a prince said, *These people are special to me and should be protected.* Or he was reading too much into it.

Tired. Marsh hadn't realized how tired he was until that moment. His legs had started to ache again, so he let his moms talk the marines' ears off and went back to the bench. Just as he leaned back against the wall and shut his eyes, a shadow loomed between him and the light. Marsh cracked one eye to find Eze Thiam from DME Services staring down at him with a dark frown.

"Hey, Eze." Marsh sat up slowly. "Um, is there a problem?"

"Problem. I suppose you could put it that way." Eze sat beside him, folding his long frame with enviable grace. "Marsh. Honest answer. How many times have you done repairs on your limbnet?"

"Between the three I've had?" Marsh wasn't sure he could remember *all* of them.

Eze made an exasperated sound. "No, your current one."

"Oh, well. Not many? Seven… no, eight times."

"Eight times." Eze's tone was sepulchral and forbidding. "And this last time was due to actual physical damage."

"Yes. It wasn't a hard fix or anyth— How did you know?"

"Your handsome prince told on you and had his staff call us." Eze tapped his stylus on Marsh's knee. "Just because you're capable of jury-rigging your failing equipment for years does *not* mean you should report it as *functional*. We talked about this last time."

"I…" Last time had been many years before. How did Eze remember that? "I suppose. But it does still work. Other people—"

"Marsh." Again the stylus tapped. "In this case, other people is you. It's wonderful that you're civic-minded. That you think of others. That's great. But your mothers report you've been in pain, and there have been incidents of sudden failure. No more excuses."

"But—"

Eze's white hair caught the light as he leaned forward. "No more, young man. You'll come with me to the fabrication labs where they're going to do scan mapping for your new limbnet."

"Don't they have my scans?"

"The Version Five is more complex and needs a new scan."

"Oh. When?"

"Now, Marsh. Right now."

Probably no arguing with that, but the timing's awful. Marsh stood with a sigh and turned to tell Shiro where he was going… only to find Shiro and his small entourage were gone.

Marsh spun in place, even though he knew looking twice wouldn't make a difference. "Where's Shiro?"

"He's…" Mama K put a hand on Marsh's arm,

her eyes shining with tears. "His mother's flagship is standing off station. Her shuttle docked a minute ago and they took Shiro to her."

"Oh." Marsh stared at the inner doors to Immigration. Back there was the access to shuttle docking. All solid, dependable, and real. But the decking had opened a yawning hole under him, and every solid surface had taken on a hazy, nightmare quality. He blinked back his own tears, or tried, but they slid down his face anyway. "He didn't even say goodbye."

SHIRO FOUGHT against his irritation at being hustled off without being able to explain to Marsh. But he wouldn't do himself any favors or win any arguments by being short with his imperial mother. He walked with his injured arm held close at the center of a mixed-marine contingent—his and his mother's—Sergeant Hana at her accustomed spot behind his right shoulder.

His mother's secondary vessel was only designated as a shuttle because it had the ability to utilize shuttle docking at most stations. Twice the size of his *Dahlia*, the *Ryu* had living quarters separate from the flight deck, including the receiving room where his escort steered him now. Shiro's mother didn't rise from the kotatsu, already set with the quilted chrysanthemum blanket and Shiro's favorite turtle and lotus tea set, but she did raise an eyebrow at him.

"Shiro-kun, you are a bit worse for wear."

Behind him, the marine contingent snapped to

attention, still as stone. They would stay that way until his mother dismissed them.

While he was excused formality in such an informal setting, he still offered a bow. "I'm well, Mama. And have been well looked after."

"Hmm." She waved to the spot across from her. "Come sit. We have things to discuss."

Playing his part of dutiful son, Shiro snuggled in with his legs under the blanket, nearly melting in the comforting warmth of the kotatsu. She poured for them both and pushed a plate of delicate shortbreads to him, both of them waiting until cookies had been nibbled and tea had been drunk.

"Judiciary informs us they have secured Mr. McClain and five mercenaries in his employ," she offered as her opening gambit. "Would you estimate that as the entire contingent onstation?"

Shiro nodded, setting his cup down carefully with shaking fingers. He hadn't realized how cold he was until he began to warm. "I never saw more than three at once. He has a ship standing off station. Possibly more than one."

She tipped him a nod. "Yes. Two ships. Both boarded by the station's authorities and grappled to station docking. One of the ships had an interesting communications device that was blocking Altairian channels. We intend to impound this device and study it. Quite interesting."

Mama's engineers would have a field day. "I should mention that Chirag Tazi and Goro Rin are also onstation."

She gave him that tiny, knowing smile all her children found irritating. "Yes. We are aware. Goro

Rin tackled McClain in the middle of one of the mercantile concourses. It was, by all accounts, a magnificent brawl, but Goro-san prevailed. Station authorities have promised to forward the vid. Chirag Tazi, whom I gather was responsible for the newscast, went a step farther and called our foreign office on Eridani Prime to inform us of your location. We have no illusions regarding his motives, but we thank him for that, nevertheless."

Well. That was something I should've thought of doing. "I think he was attempting an abduction when I stopped for fuel."

After pouring them both more tea, she gave another slight nod in acknowledgment. "Your precipitous flight from Adanai space was more than suspicious, my most worrisome child. Financial agents have been dispatched to examine some of his less-transparent transactions. We have no jurisdiction, but we have resources." She sipped delicately. "It is an interesting set of challenges you have set us, Shiro-kun."

Shiro ducked his head. "Apologies, Mama."

An imperial hand waved in dismissal. "Your only intention was time alone at the family retreat. The actions of evil-minded men are not your fault."

"I shouldn't have run from Goro Rin and Touma Saito's ships, though."

"You reacted on the limited information you had at the time. I commend you on your swift thinking when you had no one to turn to for advice." She looked away toward the outside viewing screen. "Security agents are sweeping your *Dahlia's* systems. A tracker code had been embedded in navigation. Presumably McClain's. There may have been other trespasses including probable nano-trackers in your bloodstream, which may have occurred during your fuel stop in Adanai space."

While Shiro had suspected something of the sort, to have it confirmed was still alarming. "How did he…?" Chirag had touched him. Taken his hand. It must have been then. "No. I suppose that's not important now. Are we bound home, then?" *I need to explain to Marsh. I can't just leave. I need to do* something.

"We will be in dock a few days. Negotiations regarding extradition and charges now involve three intergalactic governments. Our legal counsel is gathering data, and we await the arrival of ESTO legal and government representatives, as well. You will have ample time to thank those onstation who assisted you, especially the young man who played the part of your fictitious affianced."

"I… Mama, I need to speak to you about that, if you have a few moments."

"This time is for you alone, my Shiro." She settled with her hands in her lap, all of her intimidating attention on him.

Shiro tried to match her posture, though he knew he could never look half as regal. "It began as a fiction in a panicked moment. Perhaps even then there was a kernel of truth to it for me."

She tipped her head to the side. "Your feelings are no longer fictitious."

He couldn't keep up the posture any longer and slumped around his burned arm. "I liked him from the start. When we had spent time together, I liked him more and more. I know he's no one the imperium would consider as a partner for me on any list. And still… there it is."

"I'm pleased to hear you've made a connection with someone at last." She began slowly. Carefully it seemed to him. "You know you may choose any consort your heart desires. No one may stop you."

"I know. I do." Suddenly, the words began to spill out in a flood. "But I don't want to take Marsh as a consort and marry someone else. He's the one, the only one I've connected with, and you and I have tried over the years, oh, we've tried. I love him, Mama, and I don't want anyone else, even though I know he's not a court-appropriate or diplomatic or advantageous choice. I can't imagine having anyone else in… well, having anyone else."

Her perfectly lacquered nails drummed the quilt once. "I'm not certain you've thought this through. You cannot live entirely away from court. He must have a life here you would be ripping him from."

Shiro traced a finger around a cloth chrysanthemum. "I have. Thought it through. I have a ship. I have skills. I could apply to the Artisan's Guild for stationer status. Marsh—he's the station's only utility mechanic, and I gather that's historically not a usual thing—could train someone else to take some of the work. He could have leave time, which, apparently, he has been refusing to take. We could live here and at court when necessary. It would…" Shiro managed to look up and met her pensive frown. "It would be difficult. But not impossible."

"He would need to be genetically mapped, Shiro-kun," she said softly. "No one with genetic issues can contribute to the line. He is partially disabled, is he not?"

"An accident in utero, Mama. Not genetic."

"It's certainly not unheard of," she murmured as if to herself. "There is precedent."

He held his breath, waiting for her decision, his entire body stretched so taut prepared for argument that her next words were a shock. "I don't suppose you have asked him?"

Shiro could only gape at her, rude and inelegant. She didn't reprimand him for it, though, turning calmly to the marine contingent at the door, a calm hard-won through war, trade negotiations, and the drama stirred up by twelve children.

"Sergeant Hana, I believe it would be prudent to locate Prince Shiro's young man at this point."

MARSH SAT on his bed with Gally held tight in his lap. He needed to hold onto something or he might fly apart, molecules drifting through the ventilation system to haunt the station forever.

"It's not like I didn't *know*, Gally."

Cherep.

"I knew he'd have to leave. He's a *prince*. He can't stay here with me, living with my moms, picking limes." He choked back a sob and swiped at his eyes. Again. "I guess I thought it wouldn't be so soon. That I'd have a chance to say some things."

He'd even tried to tell himself it would hurt when Shiro left, believing that acknowledging it beforehand would make it easier. It hadn't. He had managed to get through the scan mapping at the labs without breaking down. Something to be proud of, at least. But since then, he'd hurried away from everyone and ignored his moms' concerned messages.

The door to his quarters chimed and he sighed. "I'm not up to seeing anyone. Who is it, Gally?"

His AI ferret chirped and projected an image of the other side of Marsh's door. For a moment, Marsh couldn't move. The camera must have been… *could* a camera be mistaken? He tucked Gally under his arm and went to open the door.

"Shiro?"

"Yes. Hello." Shiro took him by the shoulders and backed him up so he could come in. "I needed… Oh, no. You've been crying. I'm so sorry. My mother had to speak to me and I didn't have time and I didn't want you thinking I'd just *left* you."

The rapid, distracted speech pattern wasn't at all like Shiro. "You're not in trouble again, are you?"

Shiro blinked at him. "I'm not sure… Never mind. I needed to come back and tell you things, the most important of which I should've said first. And that would be that I love you. I have plans and I think they'll work, especially since there's a good probability that Mother supports us. It would take work, but I think we could manage everything if you married me."

It took a moment to parse, but then Marsh couldn't help a strangled laugh. "Shiro, you need to take a breath. And I think that was the *worst* proposal the galaxy has probably ever heard."

"Was it?" Shiro let go of him and sank down on

the bed. "I'm so sorry. Should I bother to try again? Or have I just made a complete idiot of myself?"

Marsh set Gally down and sat beside his anxious prince, an uncomfortable skirmish going on in his heart between wild hope and lingering despair. "You didn't. Let's take things from the beginning. You said you love me? It's only been a few days. That's what anyone sensible would say."

"It has. Yes." Shiro inhaled slowly, maybe trying to calm himself. "I know it's not sensible, but I've never felt this for anyone. I don't think time is always a factor in knowing when something—some*one*—feels just right, do you? And I do love you, Marsh."

Those words, spoken just above a hesitant whisper, sank under Marsh's skin like tiny suns, warming the echoing void that had been growing in him ever since he realized Shiro would have to return home. "I just wanted to be sure. You know I love you, too, right? In case you didn't, I do."

Shiro ducked his head, humming a little laugh. "Our declarations wouldn't win any awards today."

"Probably not." Marsh reached over to take Shiro's hand. "I'm still a little confused, so maybe you need to tell me your brilliant plans."

For the next twenty minutes, Marsh listened as Shiro mapped out every necessary action and contingency, right down to what he would create for his juried board as the last step to acceptance in the Artisan's Guild. Amazed at how Shiro had managed to research and plan so much in such a short time, the long explanation did settle Marsh. He'd been afraid Shiro was being impulsive, but a shipyard's worth of thinking had gone into his plans.

"A second utility mechanic?" Marsh frowned, stuck on that one piece more than any other. "Some days, there's not enough to keep just me busy."

Shiro nodded. "So I hear. But every department knows there's only one. So sometimes they don't take leave because there aren't enough of you. If there were two or more, not only could *you* take time off, but other mechanics could that haven't been."

"How… Are you just guessing?"

"Ah, no." Shiro cleared his throat. "I spoke to Union Scheduling. They said they keep meaning to bring it up with the Guild Council, but things kept pushing it back."

"And they told you things because you're polite and handsome."

"I'm a visiting diplomat." Shiro poked him. "They *had* to be polite back."

Marsh laughed at that. He could just see it. "But your mom. She's not going to okay any of this."

The tiniest hint of a smile tugged at Shiro's lips. "She was the one who insisted I come to talk to you about all of this."

"She was? She did?" A wave of dizzy astonishment hit so hard Marsh had to put a hand on the wall.

"She did. Are you all right?"

"I'm just… is there a better word than shocked? Exponential shock or something?"

Shiro snuggled close to rest his head on Marsh's shoulder. "She does want me to be happy, and she says there *is* precedence. With all that said—and I'm sorry, it was a lot—Marsh Kensinger will you, even though I'm a lazy, freeloading prince with no actual job yet, consider marrying me?"

"Can I think about it?" Beside him, Shiro stiffened and started to pull away. Marsh wrapped an arm around him to keep him close. "I'm joking. Sorry. Inappropriate stress humor. I would be honored to marry such a brave, resourceful, freeloading prince. Yes, Shiro. That's a yes."

"Oh thank goddess."

Shiro put a hand to the side of Marsh's face and kissed him. Between the pain in Marsh's legs and Shiro's burned arm, maybe it wasn't the most perfect, epic kiss in the history of lip-locks, but it was theirs, it was real, and now they'd have a lifetime to practice. That made it more than perfect.

CHAPTER TEN

S hiro tried to be patient while he waited, but all the people hustling back and forth were making him anxious. He wandered over to the high counter by the bar in the imperial family's common room and pulled up one of the interfaces embedded in the surface. Most messages he could ignore for now, though he highlighted the reminder for his scheduled exclusive interview with Sasha Benitsky the next day. Wouldn't do to miss *that*. Then he pulled up the message he truly wanted.

Something sharp settled on his collarbone and he turned his head to find his youngest sister, Aiko, with her chin on his shoulder. "Shouldn't you be with your man right now?"

"Hmm. Well. The dressers shooed me out." Shiro scrolled through a set of vids his mother had sent. "They claim I'm a distraction. Just because Marsh asked me to save him from them."

Aiko muffled a laugh with the back of her hand. "So what are we looking at here?"

"*I'm* going to take a look at some of the footage from Bremen."

She plopped onto the stool beside his, never one to take a hint she didn't want. "Oh, good. I've wanted to see some of this."

Shiro was muttering about his nosy little sister when a hand fell on his shoulder.

"What are you two troublemakers up to?" Noriko, the sister closest in age to him, smiled down at him.

"Trying to find a moment's peace, which apparently, I'm not allowed to have." Shiro gave her a mock scowl, but they both knew he didn't mean it.

"Oh no, no. Silly boy." Their next-oldest sister, Izumi, took the stool on his other side. "Today of all days, you're not allowed any respite from annoying friends and relations. No running off to your room to read."

He heaved an exaggerated sigh and found the vid he wanted—or rather the only one he was willing to play with sisters watching. Station Judiciary had spliced it together from several cameras, initially showing Hengist sprinting through the corridors, looking over his shoulder at every turn.

At a cross corridor just before the Five-Six concourse—Shiro recognized the bao vendor's stall in the corner of the shot—a broad-shouldered person hurtled out of the shadows and slammed into Hengist, taking him to the ground.

Shiro's sisters made varying sounds of approval and dismay as the attacker landed three punches before Hengist could even react.

"Is that..." Aiko leaned closer to the image. "Is that Lord Rin?"

"That is indeed Goro Rin," Noriko verified. She cocked her head. "I knew he was a good fencer but didn't realize he was an accomplished street brawler."

Everyone winced as Hengist landed a punch to Goro's nose. It didn't even slow him down. Blood pouring down his face, he gave no quarter, coming after Hengist mercilessly until he was sprawled unmoving on the ground. Goro might not have stopped even then, but the few merchants still on the concourse pulled him off.

"Goddesses, Shiro." Aiko shot him a look of disbelief. "*That's* the one you *rejected*?"

"He's probably more your flavor." Shiro bumped her shoulder. "Being adept at violence isn't my first criteria for a husband."

Aiko's glare at him was brief before she glanced around at their older sisters. "Will he be here today?"

"I saw his name on the guest list." Izumi waggled a hand back and forth. "He may or may not come."

"Depends on how broken his heart is still." Hachiko had joined them on silent feet. "Did you know Mother's given him a command position in the imperial guard?"

Shiro blinked up at his tallest brother. "Is that a punishment or a reward?"

"He'll see it as a reward," Noriko said with confidence. "I don't think retiring from the service and being involved with the family business has been good for him."

There was something distinctly predatory in Aiko's expression as she watched the vid replay. "Good. That means he'll be around."

Shiro wondered if he owed Goro a warning, but

he was a grown man and most likely would only feel humiliated if it came from Shiro. Still, Shiro sent up a quick prayer for his inevitable collision with Hurricane Aiko.

He dismissed the screen and turned to take in the room full of siblings, spouses, nephews, and nieces. All of his siblings wore dress uniforms in red and gold. All of them still were active service in some capacity, from Admiral Princess Tsuda, fleet ops, to Major Princess Noriko, imperial medical service, to Captain Prince Hideo, legal branch, to Cadet Princess Aiko, in her final month before graduation, and Cadet Prince Ren, starting his first year at the academy, since he would turn sixteen in a week.

They adjusted each other's collars and sashes and debated, teased, and laughed, filling the room with a joyful racket. Sometimes they were too much, and sometimes they irritated him beyond reason. But his heart warmed to see them in one place, and they were all there for him.

Noriko gave him a one-armed hug, then straightened the red-and-white-patterned formal tunic he wore. "Are you sure you're ready for this?"

He leaned his head against hers with a smile. "I am. Not even a question. I truly am."

MARSH TUGGED at the high collar of his tunic. Why were fancy clothes always so uncomfortable? Not that he thought he'd be allowed to wear coveralls for this, and the bright-blue tunic with silver leaves embroidered all over *was* beautiful, but no one wearing embroidered clothes in stories talked about how *itchy* they were.

Now that they'd finally left him alone—after manicuring, pedicuring, dressing him and redressing him like a doll until he wanted to scream—at least he could take some time to appreciate the room they'd plunked him in. Rooms. Plural. He had a whole guest suite with a sitting room, breakfast room, bedroom, and bath that was larger than his apartment back home.

The more he thought about it, the dizzier he felt. He was just a guest. What did the imperial suite look like? How many suites *were* there? Could you fit an entire city inside the palace?

He promised himself he'd sleep on one of the couches, since he'd feel lost on a bed big enough for a ping pong table. There were little snacks in the front room he wasn't sure he was supposed to eat, alcohol in crystal decanters with delicate glasses, beautiful sculpture and flower arrangements, towels as thick as pillows—and he was terrified to touch anything.

"I'll just stand here in the middle of the room until they come get me. That way I won't screw anything up."

Gally poked their nose out from under the bed skirt and galumphed over to him. The staff had put a cute bow tie around Gally's neck, one that matched Marsh's tunic perfectly. He managed a smile as Gally stood on hind legs and put a paw on his knee. *Ridiculously cute.*

The outer door opening startled him out of admiring Gally. They both turned to move toward the sitting room to see who'd arrived. *Please let it be Shiro, please.* Marsh halted at the entrance to the sitting room when he spotted his visitor, any hope that he remembered how to speak deserting him. The woman striding into the suite would've been recognizable wearing a grain sack, but here she was in a formal gown with flowing sleeves and a glittering tiara, marine guards at her back.

The empress. Marsh stood frozen, unable to recall protocols or even if there was one for this situation.

She gestured to her guard contingent. "Leave us."

When the guards had closed the doors behind them and she turned back to Marsh, he managed a bow and a whispered, "Your Imperial Majesty."

"Oh, dear."

That wasn't what he expected an empress to say. He straightened to find her looking at him with one eyebrow raised. "Your majesty?"

"That was a dreadful bow. Shiro will have to help you with those." She glided over to one of the sofas and settled with enviable grace despite the layers of heavy fabric. "Come sit with me, Marsh, and leave the titles for now. I give you leave in private."

He perched on the edge of the sofa, his heart hammering so hard she must've heard it. "Shiro tried, ma'am. What do your other kids-in-law call you in private?"

"By name, usually."

"I'm so sorry, ma'am. You're going to think I'm an idiot. But I don't know your name."

A tiny bit of a smile quirked one side of her mouth, and for a moment she looked so much like Shiro, Marsh nearly smiled in return. "On the nets,

I'm always The Empress. It's understandable. My given name is Himiko."

"Thank you."

She waved an elegantly manicured hand. "A small thing."

"May I ask you something?"

"In private? Yes. You must have questions."

Marsh ducked his head, gathering his courage before he raised his gaze to hers again. "I have to know, ma'am—Himiko—why you're allowing this. I'm not famous or wealthy or noble. Why is this okay?"

"I believe you mean in addition to my Shiro finally having a chance at happiness?"

"Yes. I know that sounds… rude. But yes."

She turned her head to look out the third-floor window where an ancient chestnut tree grew. "I do love my children, Marsh, and I have been more than concerned about Shiro. He smiles more since he met you. Laughs more. He is more himself again. But you are shrewd to ascertain that there can be additional motives to my decisions and ancillary motives. Perhaps court won't be as difficult for you as you seem to believe."

"Ah, thank you? I think."

She allowed a small nod in acknowledgment. "We have maintained good relations with the Hansa for centuries. Good, but not particularly close relations. Trade treaties and regular commerce are no substitute for personal connections. But the Hansa have no royalty, no important families, no one with accumulations of the sort of wealth that brings governmental power."

Her fingers drummed on the arm of the couch,

maybe weighing what she would say next. It sure didn't look like an invitation to interrupt, so Marsh waited, so tense his arms shivered.

"We've gone through your records," she finally continued. "Education, employment, medical. We've conducted interviews and made observations. You may not be important as most governments count *importance*, Marsh Kensinger, but you are well regarded in your community. You have earned respect. This is what I have presented to my cabinet and my court so that no one will challenge your right to be here. You are our link to the Hansa, even if this only ever comes to be true in a social sense. A cultural interpreter and intermediary, if you will."

"I see." He did, and he felt more comfortable knowing she had imperial motives as well as maternal ones. It made more sense in an empress. "I appreciate the explanation. And I'm always happy to explain what's happening in Hansa brains."

She laughed softly, and even her laugh was regal, though it was interrupted by a series of chimes.

"Does that mean it's time?" Marsh leaped to his feet, smoothing his tunic fretfully.

Himiko was kind enough not to laugh at him. "It is. Come. I'll escort you th—"

At that moment, Gally scurried out *dook-dooking* all the way from the bedroom. "Ah, this is Gally, my AI ferret companion."

"How charming!" Her regal face blossomed in an unguarded smile, and Marsh nearly swallowed his tongue as she bent and scooped Gally into her arms. "I will carry my grand-ferret, if you don't mind."

"Not at all, ma'am."

Gally, the little miscreant, gazed out with an undeniably smug air from his imperial perch as they swept through the halls with their stiff-as-starch military escort.

"THEY'RE LATE," Shiro whispered, his hands carefully folded in front of him so he wouldn't tug on his cuffs.

Noriko put a hand on his shoulder. "Breathe, Ro. They're coming. Mama comes in her own time."

He resisted steadying himself on the plinth beside him. The reception room was packed with courtiers and dignitaries who would gossip that Prince Shiro felt faint at his betrothal. "What if she's suddenly decided she doesn't like him? What if—?"

"Don't get all worked up." Izumi murmured near his ear. "You'll smudge your eyeliner. You remember what a mess my eyes were on my betrothal day?"

"Hmm. Yes. That was funny."

She poked him in the ribs, and they both fought hard against snickering. It did help, though, knowing that other siblings had been as much of a mess for their signings. Marsh had been horrified that they had to sign a contract in front of the entire court, saying it all sounded so cold and mercantile. It was, Shiro assured him, a legal necessity, as was the six-month waiting period after the betrothal signing before they could marry. The promise of a celebration and of tables groaning with food after the ceremony mollified Marsh a bit.

Attendants opened the doors to the receiving room and the herald called out, "Her Most Imperial

Majesty, Himiko Okiko Shinohara and the Honorable Marsh Kensinger."

One hand crept up to his heart. Shiro couldn't help it. Mama was always beautiful—and somehow more so, carrying a polished, bow-tied Gally—but Marsh was breathtaking. The tunic's blue was the perfect shade for him, and the loose black pants and gleaming black sandals lent him a fairy-tale aura—Shiro's own prince, stepped out of the pages of an ancient book.

Marsh's eyes were a little too wide, bouncing around the room at all the people in attendance until he found Shiro at the front of the room. Then his smile lit his face, the corners of his eyes crinkling, as he made his sure and determined way to the plinth.

"You look gorgeous," Shiro whispered as he reached for Marsh's hands.

"I'm nothing next to you." Marsh leaned in to kiss his cheek. Not entirely to script, but Shiro wasn't complaining.

One of the family's legal advocates came to the front to read the contract, though they'd gone through it previously, thoroughly, to be certain neither he nor Marsh had objections. Six-month engagement, cohabitation was acceptable, but not common property before marriage, and on and on. The advocate's voice became a drone in the background as Shiro held Marsh's hands and drank in his face, his expressions, the way he tried not to shift from foot to foot and still did sometimes.

He should've asked for a chair. Marsh's new limbnet had been perfect so far, but Shiro still worried.

Though some things he no longer worried over.

Both Hengist and Chirag were in custody, awaiting trial. They hadn't colluded, and Hengist would face the more serious charges of physically assaulting a prince of the imperial line, but it had been confirmed that Chirag had planted biotrackers on Shiro, an assault of a different sort.

Had Hengist been an Altairian citizen, his execution would already have taken place. Extradition treaties ensured he would live, but those same documents escalated his charges to treaty violations. He would be incarcerated until his advanced old age. The man who had shot Shiro, on the other hand, would never be released. Chirag could most likely buy his way out of a prison term, but since he would no longer have any interest in pursuing an engagement, Shiro found he didn't care.

I love you, Marsh mouthed with a mischievous twinkle in his eyes. Clearly, neither one of them were paying attention to the official reading.

Shiro's stomach muscles hurt, he was trying so hard not to laugh. *I love you, too.*

Behind Marsh, the advocate cleared his throat. "If his highness would be so kind?"

Ah, the reading was finished. Distractions had made the tedious droning fly. Shiro gave Marsh's hands a squeeze and slipped around him to the plinth, where the advocate held the contract—an old-fashioned paper document—steady. Shiro signed carefully and turned to hand the pen to Marsh, warmth climbing his cheeks at the heat and promise in Marsh's eyes.

Maybe an abbreviated party attendance would be a good idea.

Marsh signed and didn't even wait to hand the pen back before he pulled Shiro close for a hungry kiss.

"Hmm. Yes. A very short party visit."

"Is it scary that I'm pretty sure you're continuing a conversation from inside your head and I understand perfectly?" Marsh slid a hand around Shiro's waist with their foreheads leaned together.

"Scary?" Shiro let out a contented sigh. "No. It's wonderful."

They did manage to remain at the celebration for over an hour, much longer than Shiro thought either of them would be able to tolerate. But Izumi the engineer started talking to Marsh about station construction and utilities, and Shiro wanted to see what would happen when Aiko spotted Goro.

"She's got him cornered," Shiro murmured to Noriko.

Noriko glanced over casually. "Goddess. Literally cornered. He's so stiff and twitchy. Ease up, Aiko."

Aiko said something and backed off a step as if she'd heard.

"Maybe aggressive is what he really needs." Hachiko gave a tiny nod in their direction. "Look, he's answering. Nodding."

"Holy stars, is that a smile?" Shiro fought against staring. "It is. I've *never* seen him smile."

"Leave them be, nosy youngsters." Masako, her voice forbidding, but her eyes dancing with laughter, was suddenly among them. "Good for our baby sister. Goro-san deserves some happiness."

I am loyal, as I ever have been, Goro had said, and he had more than proven it. Maybe Aiko was just looking for a conquest. The romantic part of Shiro's heart hoped it might be something more.

Shiro searched for Marsh, still chatting, both he and Izumi sketching on her holo tablet. He raised an eyebrow in question, and Marsh nodded as he gave Izumi his apologies and made his way through the guests to Shiro. For her part, Izumi calculated his trajectory immediately. She grinned and raised a hand in a cheeky wave.

"Go, Shiro-kun." Masako gave him a tiny shove in Marsh's direction. "The Minister of Arts is on a collision course and she'll never let you escape. We will run interference."

Good as Masako's word, the siblings closed in. Shiro caught Marsh's hand as soon as he was in reach. They didn't quite run from the reception, but it was a close thing, Gally galumphing as fast as they could to catch up.

"How do you live like this?" Marsh scrubbed his hands over his face when they'd reached the safety of Shiro's bedroom.

"You don't like my suite?" Shiro thought he had an inkling of what Marsh meant and told himself sternly that this wasn't the time for hurt feelings.

Marsh plunked onto the padded bench at the end of Shiro's bed. "Everything's so huge, so open, so much. I never *thought* I had a problem with open spaces. Apparently, I do."

Oh. Shiro knelt in front of him and took his hands gently. "I can have the suite remodeled. Make a smaller space in here for you if you want one. I want you to be comfortable here. At home."

"No, no. I'll get used to it. I don't want to make extra work for people." Marsh heaved a shuddering sigh. "I'll be all right as long as… There isn't staff coming to *un*dress us, is there?"

"There won't be. I gave them the night off." Shiro kissed each of Marsh's fingers in turn, hoping to distract him from his discomfort. "You don't ever have to accept help. You have every right to say no. But the dressers are helpful for formal functions and for assistance in what's appropriate for everyday activities around the palace, too."

"Okay. Good to know." Marsh leaned forward to kiss his forehead. "You're being so patient with me. I feel like I don't know anything here. Though I do like your kinda scary family. Might even get all their names straight one day."

"They are a lot to take in. I like your family, too, very much. I'm sorry your mothers weren't here." Shiro pulled Marsh to his feet and wrapped him in a tight hug, ignoring for the moment how good Marsh felt pressed tight against him. Mostly ignoring.

Marsh hummed against the skin of Shiro's throat and kissed him just under his ear. "We'll see them soon. Mama D just was not having any part of *some fancy contract signing* when we're having our domestic partnership ceremony there."

"Marsh… love…" Shiro cleared his throat. "I can't guarantee I'll be careful with your clothes if you keep kissing me there."

"Sorry." Marsh chuckled and set him back. "I should go, ah, get myself ready."

"Ready?"

The tops of Marsh's ears turned that deep red Shiro loved. "I'd like you inside me tonight. And with the dressers around before, I couldn't really get myself ready for your cock."

Shiro smiled and smoothed his hands down Marsh's arms. "Oh, that sort of ready. Bathroom is over there. You should find everything you want in the cabinet by the sink."

He did help Marsh out of the stiffly embroidered tunic. Beautiful needlework, but Marsh looked so relieved to be out of it that Shiro decided to have a word with the tailors for future garments.

While Marsh was in the bathroom, Shiro undressed and laid their clothes carefully over a chair. Gally had already curled up in sleep mode, so he didn't feel self-conscious about wandering around naked. Not that Gally cared about naked people, but they were an intelligent being. It felt wrong.

Marsh called from the bathroom, "Why are there so many towels? Are there different towels for different things? Like with forks?"

After a deep breath, Shiro was confident he could keep the laughter from his voice. "Use whatever you like. There are no wrong towels."

"You're laughing at me."

"No." Shiro took another deep breath. "A little." And another breath. "I love you."

Grumbling came from the bathroom, but a moment later Marsh stepped out, gloriously naked. He saw where Shiro had hung things and added the rest of his clothes to the pile, carefully straightening each piece.

"Come choose."

Shiro held his hand out and walked Marsh over to the wooden chest on a side bureau. A wave of sudden shyness threatened to overcome him, but this was Marsh, who needed to see every part of him. He ran his fingertips over the carvings of birds and dragons, then opened the lid.

"Nice." Marsh leaned over the chest. "Do you have a favorite cock?"

"Depends on my mood. I want you to pick one you like."

"Bossy." Marsh picked out the one with the most natural shape, veins and all. "This one."

Shiro kissed his shoulder, snatched up Marsh's selection, and tugged him toward the bed. Both impatient, they reached for each other at the same time and landed on the covers in a tangled heap. Marsh wriggled back onto the featherbed with little sounds of pleasure as he hitched his head onto the pillows and sprawled out on his back.

"It's so soft."

"Haven't you tried the one in your suite yet?" Shiro tipped his head to the side, taking in the beautiful length of Marsh as he shook his head slowly, appearing for once as indolent and relaxed as a housecat. "Ah. I thought you might have taken a nap, at least, since we arrived. They'll move your things in here, though. Now that we're official."

Marsh grinned. "So us screwing around is sanctioned?"

"It is." Shiro kept his cock firmly in hand and crawled over until he could lower himself atop Marsh, humming and shivering in pleasure at the sudden contact of heated skin on skin. "You're not my *pretend* fiancé anymore, love."

"All signed and legal." Marsh wrapped both arms around him and hugged him tight. "I'm not going to admit how many times I wished it wasn't pretend, but it just seemed ridiculous to think about."

"Hmm. Like a fairy tale. I'm not going to admit that, either. Even if it is true."

Shiro wriggled happily and set his knees on either side of Marsh's hips. Leaning in slowly, he kissed Marsh in soft, butterfly touches until it became too much and too little for them both. They crashed together, lips, tongues, and teeth, magma heat pooling in Shiro's core until he wondered if the bed would catch fire. This man—*this man*—held him and stroked him, and Shiro didn't shy away, didn't have to talk himself into being touched. He yearned toward Marsh's wonderful hands, hungered for more of his touch.

He broke off to suck on Marsh's neck, nibbling down to lick at his collarbone. With his free hand, he coaxed one of Marsh's knees up and reached underneath, stroking the firm globe of Marsh's ass. He slid a hand between Marsh's cheeks, his heart leaping at Marsh's gasp when his finger found Marsh's entrance, all lubed up as he'd hoped.

"Told you… I was getting ready," Marsh panted, gripping Shiro's arms hard enough to leave indentations.

"Very thorough. I like that," Shiro murmured as he got his cock settled. A squeeze just under the head triggered a clever reservoir that sent lube up to the tip, which he spread over the top third. *No such thing as too much lube.* To Marsh, he whispered, "Ready?"

Marsh hooked a leg over Shiro's shoulder. "Yes, but about to die of waiting any second now."

"And here I thought you were such a patient man," Shiro tried to say sternly, completely ruined by a snicker. "Just tell me if being folded like this gets uncomfortable. I don't want to hurt you."

"You won't, sweetheart. The new limbnet is so much better." Marsh smiled up at him, his voice softer now. "Just go slow."

Whatever you need. Always. Shiro eased his cock inside, though it was an easy glide with all of Marsh's prep. Tempting to stare down at that connection between them, watch himself sinking into Marsh, but he kept his eyes on Marsh's face the entire time—how his neck arched and his eyes fluttered shut on a soft gasp.

When Shiro drew Marsh's other leg up onto his shoulder, those dark eyes flew open.

"Gah… Shiro… Yes! There, right there. Oh, stars. Right. *There.*"

Marsh began to rock along with Shiro's thrusts, his words unhinging entirely into sharp gasps of pleasure, the movements hitting all the right spots for Shiro, too, in a swift climb from pleasure to sparks shooting through him with every thrust.

Orgasm snuck up on him faster than he anticipated, and he came with a sharp *ha* and a drawn-out moan as he continued grinding into Marsh. He reached over to grab Marsh's cock, never slowing down as he matched the pumping of his hand with his hips.

"Shiro… Shiro…" Marsh arched and cried out, no more words, just the achingly beautiful sound of his moans as he shot pearly white over his chest and belly.

Slowly, Shiro calmed his movements, gentled his grip, letting them come down together until they were both still, his head resting on Marsh's shoulder.

"Oh, yes," he murmured finally. "More of *that*, please."

Marsh's laugh was nearly soundless. "Anytime. Well, maybe not *any*time, like in public, but you know what I mean. More of that and all the other things."

"Hmm. I like the sound of that."

Shiro snuggled next to Marsh for a few minutes before he scrambled from the bed to clean them both up. While he was putting things away, a stray thought poked at him. "Marsh?"

"Mmm."

"Did you have a chance to read *Newt's Garden* yet?"

Marsh scooted up to lean against the mound of pillows against the headboard. "We've been a little busy? No, not yet."

"Do you want me to read it to you?" Shiro returned to the bed and snuggled in, pulling the covers over both of them.

"I'd love it if you'd read to me." Marsh rolled to rest his head on Shiro's chest, one arm wrapped around his waist. "For that book, though, it depends. Does it have a happy ending? I don't think I want anything without a happy ending right now."

Shiro sat up a little farther, gesturing at the controls on the bedpost to turn on his holo reader. "That's a little spoilery, don't you think?"

"Don't care," Marsh mock grumped.

"It does. Have a happy ending. At least I thought so."

"All right. Then, yes. Please."

After a moment's searching, he found the story in his recent reads, put an arm around Marsh to pull him closer, and began, "*Some version of spring had returned the day Newt finally unwrapped his carefully hoarded seeds…*"

As he read, he smiled, revisiting Newt's meeting with Frog and all that lay before them. The setting was terribly sad, the struggle wasn't easy, but Shiro had wanted so badly to share this story of the triumph of hope and determination with his Stationbookworm. Now he was, and the sharing was so much better than he'd ever imagined.

He understood what Marsh meant, about happy endings. Maybe later, he would read other things again, but for now, in this state of warmth and joy, with someone who truly loved him by his side, only happy endings would do.

Sincerely,
Mischief Corner Books

ABOUT ANGEL MARTINEZ

Angel Martinez is the pen name of a writer of several genres who writes *both* kinds of queer fiction – Science Fiction and Fantasy. (What? There are others?) Currently living part time in the hectic sprawl of northern Delaware, (and full time inside the author's head) Angel has one husband, one son, at least one cat at any given time, a changing variety of other furred and scaled companions, a love of all things beautiful and a terrible addiction to the consumption of both knowledge and chocolate.

For more information on Angel's work, please visit:

Official Website:
http://angelmartinezauthor.weebly.com/

Email:
angelmartinezauthor@gmail.com

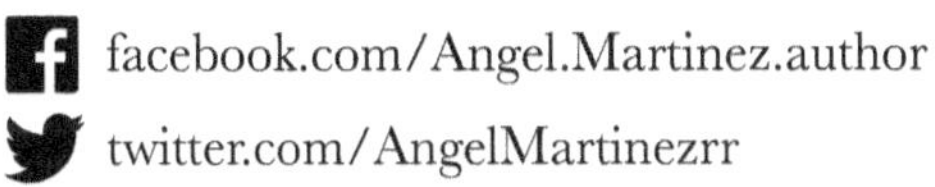

facebook.com/Angel.Martinez.author

twitter.com/AngelMartinezrr

ALSO BY ANGEL MARTINEZ

BRANDYWINE INVESTIGATIONS

Brandywine Investigations: Open for Business (Omnibus)

Brandywine Investigations: Family Matters (Omnibus)

BRIMSTONE

Potato Surprise #1

Hell for the Company #2

Fear of Frogs #3

Shax's War #4

Beside a Black Tarn #5

The Brimstone Journals: Collection One

The Brimstone Journals: Collection Two

The Hunt for Red Fluffy #6

The Brimstone Journals: Collection Three

A Fine Mess #7

THE ENDANGERED FAE SERIES

Finn

Diego

Semper Fae

No Fae is an Island

ESTO UNIVERSE

Vassily the Beautiful

Prisoner 374215

A Matter of Faces

Gravitational Attraction

Sub Zero

By Imperial Decree

LIJUN Trilogy (with Freddy Mackay)

Fireworks & Stolen Kisses

Trysts & Burning Embers

Detonations & Devotion (TBD)

INTERPLANETARY MULTISPECIES PACT (IMP)**

A Christmas Cactus for the General

A Message from the Home Office

*******SHARED UNIVERSE*

The Nut Job by Freddy MacKay

THE PUDDING PROTOCOLS UNIVERSE

Safety Protocols for Human Holidays

The Solstice Pudding

The Anti-Quest (Holiday 2020)

THE WEB OF ARCANA

The Mage on the Hill

OFFBEAT CRIMES

Lime Gelatin and Other Monsters

Pill Bugs of Time

Skim Blood & Savage Verse

Feral Dust Bunnies

Jackalopes & Woofen-Poofs

All the World's an Undead Stage

SINGLE TITLES

Eating Stars

Yule Planet

The Color of His Crest

Hearts & Flowers: A Tale of Hay Fever and Bad Decor

Boots

The Line

AURA UNIVERSE (with Bellora Quinn)

Quinn's Gambit

Flax's Pursuit

Kellen's Awakening